Logan
Arnold

BUILDING THE MAGICAL WORLD

Written by Elizabeth Dowsett

Sorting Hat

Minifigure sits or stands on chair to be Sorted into a house

Disk spins

Disk printed with the symbol of each house

Bar indicates chosen house when disk stops

THE SORTING HAT (SET 4701)

Contents

The Great Hall

First of three Hagrid minifigures

First of four Dumbledore minifigures

First of five Snape minifigures

Peeves the poltergeist

HAGRID'S HUT (SET 4707)

SNAPE'S CLASS (SET 4705)

Harry wearing the Sorting Hat

THE SORTING HAT (SET 4701)

Chapter 2:
Beyond the Brick

Gryffindor Tower

First of eight Draco Malfoy minifigures

Fluffy the three-headed dog

The Mirror of Erised has a lenticular image of Harry

Devil's Snare

HOGWARTS CASTLE (SET 4709)

FORBIDDEN CORRIDOR (SET 4706)

THE FINAL CHALLENGE (SET 4702)

Main hall piece can break apart into three separate sections

Owl from the Owlery

Colorful, transparent bricks give stained-glass effect

Mechanized pendulum is connected to clock face and gate

PROFESSOR DUMBLEDORE

HOGWARTS CASTLE (SET 4757)

DEMENTOR

DEMENTOR

Gryffindor crest marks Gryffindor Tower

Introduction

LEGO® Harry Potter™ combines one of the world's favorite toys with the most successful movie franchise of all time. This combination presented LEGO designers with the kind of challenge they love—to recreate the wizarding world of the Harry Potter films in bricks. They drew upon their experience of creating LEGO favorites such as trains, ships, castles, and dragons, and used that knowledge as a starting point in visualizing the wizarding world that fans had grown to know and love.

LEGO Harry Potter can also lay claim to some important "firsts." The double-sided minifigure head was first seen on Professor Quirrell, and is now used across all LEGO themes. Similarly, Snape's 2001 minifigure had the first glow-in-the-dark head.

LEGO designers have created a world that is recognizably Harry Potter, but is also consistent with LEGO bricks. It is a world with enormous play potential as well as collectability. Come and explore the magical world of LEGO Harry Potter.

DATA BOXES

Throughout the book, sets are identified with two types of data box (see below). These give the official name of the set, the year it was first released, its identification number, the number of LEGO pieces it contains, and the movies on which it is based. The larger Data File also lists the set's components and minifigures.
The movies have the following abbreviations:
Harry Potter and the Sorcerer's Stone: I (SS)
Harry Potter and the Chamber of Secrets: II (COS)
Harry Potter and the Prisoner of Azkaban: III (POA)
Harry Potter and the Goblet of Fire: IV (GOF)
Harry Potter and the Order of the Phoenix: V (OOTP)
Harry Potter and the Half-Blood Prince: VI (H-BP)
Harry Potter and the Deathly Hallows—Part I (VII DHP1)

SET NAME	Hogwarts Castle	
YEAR 2004	NUMBER	4757
PIECES 944	FILMS	III (POA)

DATA FILE

SET NAME: Hogwarts Castle
YEAR: 2004   SET NUMBER: 4757
PIECES: 944   FILMS: III (POA)

COMPONENTS:
Main Hall; Gryffindor Tower; gatehouse;
2 owls; 3 spiders; rat; frog; bat

MINIFIGURES:
9 (Harry Potter, Hermione Granger,
Ron Weasley, Draco Malfoy,
Professor Dumbledore,
Professor Trelawney,
2 Dementors, white skeleton).

HARRY POTTER   **RON WEASLEY**   **HERMIONE GRANGER**

Timeline

THE LEGO Group released its first LEGO® Harry Potter™ sets in 2001 to coincide with the release of the movie *Harry Potter and the Sorcerer's Stone*. Ten years later, LEGO Harry Potter is still going strong with 50 sets created.

4701 The Sorting Hat ▶

◀ 4702 The Final Challenge

4704 The Chamber ▶
of the Winged Keys

◀ 4705 Snape's Class

4706 Forbidden Corridor ▶

◀ 4707 Hagrid's Hut

4708 Hogwarts Express ▶

◀ 4709 Hogwarts Castle

4721 Hogwarts Classrooms ▶

◀ 4722 Gryffindor House

4723 Diagon Alley Shops ▶

◀ 4711 Flying Lesson

4712 Troll on the Loose ▶

◀ 4714 Gringotts Bank

4726 Quidditch ▶
Practice

▲ 4727 Aragog in the
Dark Forest

◀ 4730 Chamber
of Secrets

◀ 4733 The Dueling Club

4735 Slytherin ▶

▲ 4719 Quality Quidditch
Supplies

▲ 4720 Knockturn Alley

4728 Escape from ▶
Privet Drive

◀ 4729
Dumbledore's
Office

4731 Dobby's Release ▲

◀ 4695 Mini Knight Bus

4750 Draco's Encounter with Buckbeak ▶

◀ 4751 Harry and the Marauder's Map

4752 Professor Lupin's Classroom ▶

4753 Sirius Black's Escape ▶

◀ 4754 Hagrid's Hut

4755 Knight Bus ▶

◀ 4756 Shrieking Shack

4757 Hogwarts Castle ▶

◀ 4758 Hogwarts Express

10132 Motorized ▶ Hogwarts Express

▲ 4762 Rescue from the Merpeople

▲ 4766 Graveyard Duel

▲ 4767 Harry and the Hungarian Horntail

▲ 4768 The Durmstrang Ship

4736 Freeing Dobby ▶

◀ 4737 Quidditch Match

Have it ↑

4738 Hagrid's Hut

Have it ↑

▲ 4840 The Burrow

↑ *Cool*

4841 Hogwarts Express ▲

▲ 4842 Hogwarts Castle

↑ *Have it*

▲ 5378 Hogwarts Castle

▲ 10217 Diagon Alley

↑ *Awesome*

▲ 4865 The Forbidden Forest

▲ 4866 The Knight Bus

▲ 4867 Hogwarts

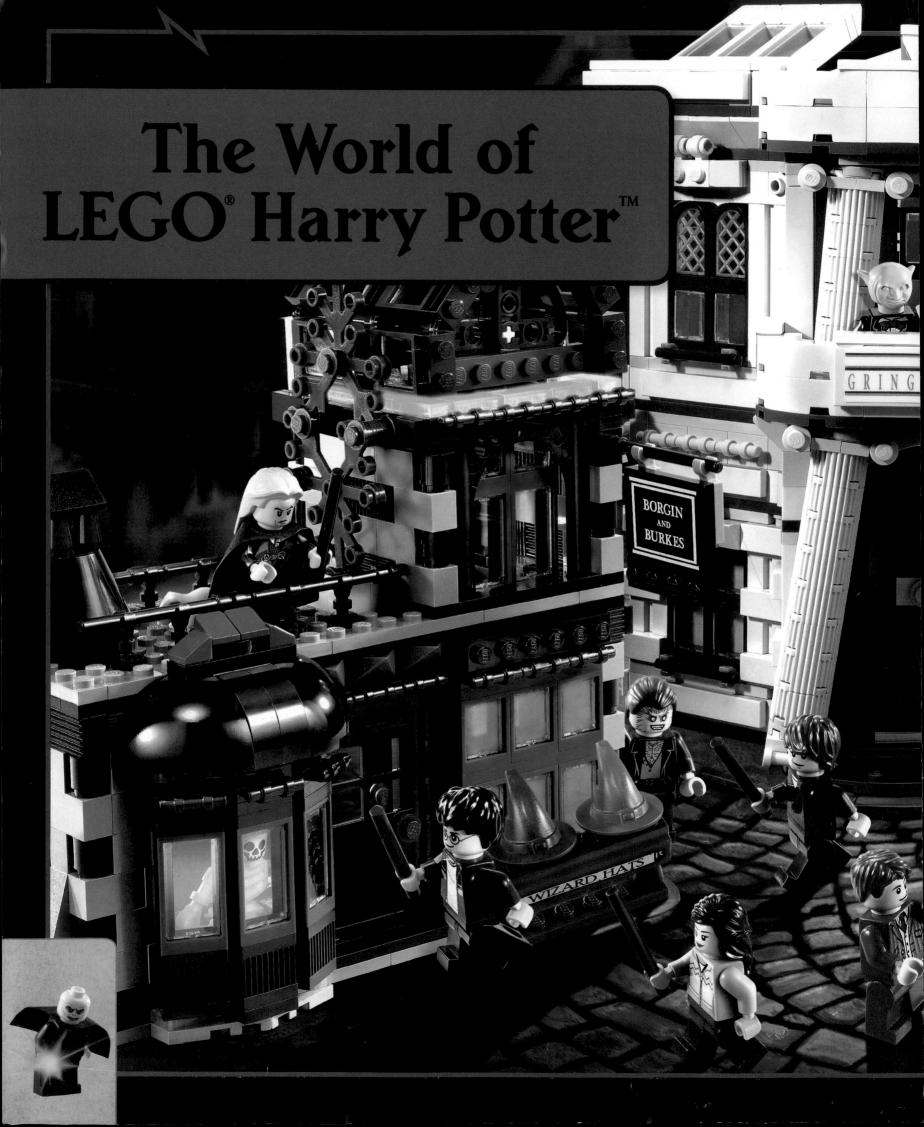

The World of
LEGO® Harry Potter™

BORGIN
AND
BURKES

GRING

WIZARD HATS

Harry Potter

SINCE 2001, 24 different Harry minifigures have been created. Some are in Gryffindor uniform, some are casually dressed, some are in Quidditch robes, but all have his trademark round glasses and lightning-shaped scar.

Originally Harry had a brown LEGO wand

HARRY POTTER (2001)

The original Gryffindor uniform has a scarlet and gold colored striped tie, colored neckline, and Gryffindor House badge. This Harry minifigure, with a black cloak, comes with eight LEGO sets.

When the chimney stack turns, letters drop down into room

NUMBER FOUR PRIVET DRIVE

► Number Four Privet Drive

This Muggle house is where Harry lives with Aunt Petunia, Uncle Vernon, and Dudley Dursley. This set also shows the scene from the second movie when Ron arrives in the Weasleys' flying car (see also page 12) to take Harry to The Burrow.

SET NAME	Escape from Privet Drive	
YEAR	2002	NUMBER 4728
PIECES	278	FILMS II (COS)

Black wand **Weird**

Brick printed with house number "4"

Set comes with three letters

Yellow Face

HARRY POTTER (2001)

This Harry minifigure, dressed in Muggle clothes, is unique to this set.

Window frame pulled out by the Weasleys' flying car

The cupboard under the stairs

VERNON DURSLEY

Uncle Vernon's face includes a ginger-colored mustache. His clothing is based on what he wears in the movies.

INVISIBILITY CLOAK

◄ Invisible Harry

In 2010, the LEGO Group created one of the three Deathly Hallows—the Invisibility Cloak, which comes with Hogwarts Castle (set 4842) and Hogwarts Express (set 4841).

Hogwarts badge

SORTING HAT

HARRY POTTER (2001)

When Harry first arrives at Hogwarts, he has not been Sorted into Gryffindor so his minifigure from The Sorting Hat (set 4701) wears a Hogwarts badge rather than a Gryffindor badge.

Lightning-shaped scar

▼ Boy Wizard

In 2004, the Gryffindor uniform torso changed to reflect the updated costumes in the films. Instead of a house badge and color around the tie, the sweater now has a plain v-neck and a colored stripe at the bottom. This torso was used until a redesign in 2010. This 2007 version of Harry in his school uniform comes only with Hogwarts Castle (set 5378).

Harry's pet owl, Hedwig

The color of the cloak differs in two of the minifigures released in 2001. This violet-cloaked Harry appears in Forbidden Corridor (set 4706), Hogwarts Castle (set 4709), and Hogwarts Classrooms (set 4721).

HARRY POTTER (2001)

Transparent neon cone piece for light

Marauder's Map tile piece

Tousled hair piece reflects Harry's unruly hair

In *Harry Potter and the Marauder's Map* (set 4751), Harry explores Hogwarts using *Lumos* to shine light from his wand.

YULE BALL HARRY

Harry wears his formal dress robes to the Yule Ball in *Harry Potter and the Goblet of Fire*. So, when it came to creating an exclusive Harry Potter minifigure for DK's *LEGO Harry Potter Building the Magical World*, LEGO designers chose Harry in his formal dress robes.

HARRY POTTER (2004)

▼ Harry's Family

In one half of Hogwarts Classrooms (set 4721), Harry's minifigure discovers the Mirror of Erised. The stickered picture here shows Harry reunited with his parents, James and Lily Potter. The other half of the set shows Harry in the Potions classroom (see page 38).

2004 Gryffindor torso

Corner of Hogwarts castle

Chrome gold decoration

James Potter

Lily Potter

SET NAME	Hogwarts Classrooms	
YEAR 2001		NUMBER 4721
PIECES 73		FILMS 1 (SS)

HARRY POTTER (2007)

HOGWARTS CLASSROOM

Clawed feet

Ron Weasley

- Bowl-shaped hair piece
- Raised eyebrow
- Ron's wand is brown
- Gryffindor torso that first appeared in 2004 has a stripe but no house badge

RON WEASLEY (2005)

RON WEASLEY is best friends with Harry Potter and Hermione Granger. There are now ten Ron Weasley minifigures, and 2010 saw the introduction of more of the Weasley clan: his parents, Molly and Arthur, his brothers, Fred and George, for the first time—and an update of his sister Ginny's minifigure.

▼ The Weasleys' Flying Car

- Chrome-effect grille
- Trunk opens

Cooler

WEASLEYS' FLYING CAR (2002)

SET NAME	Escape from Privet Drive	
YEAR	2002	NUMBER 4728
PIECES	278	FILMS II (COS)

Two versions of the Weasleys' flying car have been made in LEGO bricks. The first appears in Escape from Privet Drive (set 4728).

This Ron minifigure comes with Escape from Privet Drive (set 4728) and Hogwarts Express (set 4708)

RON WEASLEY (2001)

The second flying car, from Hogwarts Express (set 4841), has a more streamlined design.

- Roof lifts off
- A 2010 Ron minifigure
- New curved detail

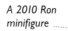

WEASLEYS' FLYING CAR (2010)

SET NAME	Hogwarts Express	
YEAR	2010	NUMBER 4841
PIECES	646	FILMS II (COS)

▲ Ron's Minifigure

The LEGO Group has created four Ron minifigures dressed in the Gryffindor uniform. This one, from 2005, is the third. For the first time, Ron has an alternative expression: His head turns around to reveal a sleeping face. This minifigure comes with Rescue from the Merpeople (set 4762) from 2005 and in Hogwarts Castle (set 5378) from 2007.

▼ Gryffindor Dormitory

This corner of Hogwarts, where Ron sleeps, makes up one half of Gryffindor House (set 4722), along with the Gryffindor common room (see page 34).

Cardboard backdrop with stone effect

► Fellow Gryffindor

Like Harry, Ron wears the red and yellow badge of Gryffindor house. His lopsided smile and freckles are captured in this specially designed face that is exclusive to Ron and appears on six of his ten minifigures.

Facial expression is unique to Ron's minifigure

RON WEASLEY (2001)

Starry printed cloak matches stars on bed canopy

BRICK FACTS

Ron inherits his family's rat, Scabbers. This LEGO rat piece appears in many of the LEGO Harry Potter sets that include Ron's minifigure.

Cupboard stands on four pink cones

SET NAME	Gryffindor House	
YEAR 2001	NUMBER	4722
PIECES 68	FILMS	1 (SS)

DORMITORY

LEGO hair piece is seen only on Ginny Weasley

MOLLY WEASLEY (2010)

Molly has a large printed apron over her house clothes in The Burrow (set 4840).

ARTHUR WEASLEY (2010)

Arthur also comes with The Burrow (set 4840). He has a hair piece the same shape as his sons', Fred and George.

FRED AND GEORGE WEASLEY (2011)

Just like in the movies, Fred and George's minifigures are identical, except for their slightly different facial expressions. The twins come with Diagon Alley (set 10217), the street that hosts their joke shop, Weasleys' Wizard Wheezes.

GINNY WEASLEY (2002)

Ginny first appears in LEGO bricks in the Chamber of Secrets (set 4730) when she is a first-year Gryffindor.

GINNY WEASLEY (2010)

Ginny now looks much older than her first minifigure, with longer, more sophisticated hair.

Harry to the Rescue

HARRY POTTER (2010)

This Harry minifigure is unique to this set. Harry is wearing the same blue jacket as Harry in Hogwarts Express (set 4841), but here he wears black instead of gray trousers.

Harry's face comes with two sides: a grinning face for the Weasleys; and a determined one for facing the attack by the Death Eaters.

DATA FILE

SET NAME: The Burrow
YEAR: 2010   **SET NUMBER:** 4840
PIECES: 568   **FILMS:** VI (H-BP)

COMPONENTS:
Three-story house; piece of marshland with reeds and catapult; mechanical fireplace

MINIFIGURES:
6 (Harry Potter, Molly Weasley, Arthur Weasley, Ginny Weasley, Bellatrix Lestrange, Fenrir Greyback)

The Quibbler newspaper on the attic window seat

Weasley family photos

Handle turns to tilt fireplace

DEATH EATERS ATTACK

In this set, danger lurks in the marshes. This LEGO® catapult helps the Death Eater minifigures Bellatrix Lestrange and Fenrir Greyback launch flaming torches.

Flaming torch

Reeds are tall enough to hide a minifigure

The Floo Network

In The Burrow, a mechanical fireplace creates the illusion of a minifigure disappearing through the Floo Network. One turn of the handle tilts the minifigure and reveals the emerald flames of burning Floo powder. Turning the handle back restores the back of the hearth and the original flames—and the minifigure is gone.

← Awesome

Poster of the Chudley Cannons Quidditch team

The Burrow

THIS SET recreates the home of the Weasley family, and is made up of a large model of the house, a fireplace, some marshland, and six minifigures: Harry Potter, Arthur, Molly, and Ginny Weasley, and two unwelcome Death Eaters, Bellatrix Lestrange and Fenrir Greyback.

◀ Wizard Home

The Burrow's crooked structure posed a challenge to LEGO designers. The team created a stable shell that is simple to build. They then added asymmetrical elements and planks to the exterior to give the impression of a lop-sided structure.

BRICK FACTS

In this set, a small green frog lives among the reeds, but in other LEGO Harry Potter sets it has different roles. In Diagon Alley Shops (set 4723), it is a potion ingredient intended for the cauldron, and in Hogwarts Express (set 4841), a brown variant is used as a Chocolate Frog for a tasty snack.

THE BURROW—FRONT

▶ Interiors

The Burrow model has three stories, but the focal point is the kitchen. The set holds a variety of details, from food to wizarding gadgets and Muggle artifacts collected by Arthur Weasley.

Bunk beds

Light fitting spins

Grandfather clock

Stacked dinner plates

Cabinets contain food

Harry's owl, Hedwig

Harry's trunk

Goblets

THE BURROW—BACK

Broomstick

Chairs swivel

Printed brick of the Daily Prophet newspaper with the breakout from Azkaban as the main story.

Hermione Granger

THERE ARE nine Hermione minifigures across all the LEGO Harry Potter sets. Seven of them wear variations of her Hogwarts uniform, the other two, in casual clothes, are from 2001 and 2011.

◄ Gryffindor

This minifigure shows the Gryffindor school uniform from the 2007 releases. Instead of a school badge, each minifigure has a stripe on their clothes in the Gryffindor colors. Like Hermione's minifigure in Rescue from the Merpeople (set 4762), her head is double-sided, with one happy face and one sleeping face.

▼ School Supplies

This small starter set named Diagon Alley Shops (set 4723) comes with just one minifigure—a unique Hermione Granger in blue clothing (see below).

Only Hermione

Potions

Pets for sale

Wizard robes

Cash register

DIAGON ALLEY

Books hinge open

Dried scorpion

SET NAME	Diagon Alley Shops	
YEAR 2001		NUMBER 4723
PIECES 80		FILMS 1 (SS)

Minifigure's accessory is a broomstick

HERMIONE GRANGER (2007)

HERMIONE GRANGER (2001)
Hermione is casually dressed to shop in Diagon Alley Shops (set 4723). She comes with a cloak and broom.

HERMIONE GRANGER (2001)
This is an original uniform from 2001. It appears in the Forbidden Corridor (set 4706) and Hogwarts Castle (set 4709) sets.

HERMIONE GRANGER (2004)
This version of Hermione is unique to Hogwarts Castle (set 4757). It is one of two figures that has an image of her Time-Turner.

Dobby

DOBBY HAS been made as two LEGO® minifigures. Both have a human torso and arms, but also a specially molded house-elf head. House-elves are shorter than humans, so Dobby has short unposeable legs.

Sock with Gryffindor shield

DOBBY (2002)
Dobby's first head is molded but unpainted. His clothing is printed onto a monochrome minifigure.

▼ Dobby (2010)

Dobby's second minifigure has printed details on his head that further represent Dobby from the films. He also has variations in the color of his body pieces, and his head and arms are now flesh-colored.

▼ Dobby's Release (2002)

Dobby comes in two sets, which both recreate the moment when Harry Potter tricks Lucius Malfoy into giving Dobby his freedom. The first set includes Dobby, Lucius, and a corner of Hogwarts castle.

Brick slides across to hide shelf

Compartment under hinged seat

SET NAME	Dobby's Release	
YEAR	2002	NUMBER 4731
PIECES	70	FILMS II (COS)

LUCIUS MALFOY (2002)

Sock is hidden inside Tom Riddle's diary

HOGWARTS

▼ Freeing Dobby (2010)

This set is the second model that depicts the moment when Dobby is freed. The set comes with Dobby, Lucius Malfoy, Harry Potter, and an archway from Hogwarts that is in keeping with the castle's architecture.

Brick slides out to knock over Lucius Malfoy

HOGWARTS

Distinctive Lucius Malfoy blond hair piece

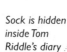

LUCIUS MALFOY (2010)

SET NAME	Freeing Dobby	
YEAR	2010	NUMBER 4736
PIECES	73	FILMS II (COS)

DOBBY (2010)

Hogwarts Express (2001)

THE LEGO Group has been designing train sets since 1966, so in 2001, it brought its rail expertise to the Hogwarts Express. Since then, four versions of the train have been released, the first in 2001, two in 2004, and one in 2010.

In this set, Harry and Ron's minifigures are in Muggle clothing for their first journey to Hogwarts. Only Hermione appears in her Hogwarts school uniform.

HARRY POTTER (2001)

No panes in windows so minifigures can lean out

Bench   *Table*   *Luggage*

HOGWARTS EXPRESS™

▲ Passenger Car

The set's designers thought carefully about the look and playability of the first passenger car and its design lasted for the next two sets. The carriage has a layer of mostly smooth tiles below the windows so that the upper part can be removed easily. The coach has two compartments, each with a table and benches for two minifigures.

▼ Locomotive

Set 4708, the first of the four Hogwarts Express trains, set the precedent for the look of the scarlet locomotive, number "5972." It is based on the visualization of the train in the first movie, *Harry Potter and the Sorcerer's Stone.*

Piece is printed with "Hogwarts Express"

Upper part is hinged

FLYING LUGGAGE

In this set, the engine of the Hogwarts Express stows luggage and has a mechanical unloading feature. When you release the lever, the luggage pops out onto the platform.

Stowed luggage flies out of here

Lever

Trunk with chrome-finished key

▼ King's Cross Station

This set comes with a two-sided model of King's Cross Station. One side shows the "Muggle" station with signs for platforms 9 and 10. The other side of the model—which is accessed through a revolving door in the middle of the wall—is platform 9¾.

Revolving door

PLATFORMS 9 AND 10

Stickered sign

Station clock

RON WEASLEY (2001)

As Ron's minifigure sets off for his first year at Hogwarts, he carries his pet rat, Scabbers, and a LEGO suitcase.

Ornate railing

Hedwig

Harry Potter

Revolving door

Old-fashioned style lampposts

Ron Weasley

PLATFORM 9¾

Hogwarts Express (2004)

TWO HOGWARTS Express sets were released in 2004. The first (set 4758) is a reworking of the original design (set 4708), and the second (set 10132) is a motorized version.

▶ Hogsmeade

The original Hogwarts Express set from 2001 (set 4708) comes with King's Cross —the train's departure point. This set introduces its destination—the platform at the village station of Hogsmeade.

▼ Train Set

The engine and passenger car of this set are similar in design to the original Hogwarts Express (set 4708, see pages 18–19), but they come with two new characters from the third movie: a Dementor and Professor Lupin.

DATA FILE

SET NAME: Hogwarts Express
YEAR: 2004   SET NUMBER: 4758
PIECES: 389   FILMS: III (POA)

COMPONENTS:
Locomotive engine; passenger car; Hogsmeade platform; owl; rat

MINIFIGURES:
4 (Harry Potter, Ron Weasley, Professor Lupin, Dementor)

HOGSMEADE PLATFORM

Professor Lupin with chocolate bar

Grille piece

Second steam stack

Sticker with train's number "5972"

Stickered decoration

Model includes 18 spoked wheels

Magnet piece to attach to other cars

BRICK FACTS

Among the school supplies that minifigures must have for their third year is *The Monster Book of Monsters*. The piece has a fierce face to reflect how it snaps viciously in the films.

▼ Motorized Train

This is the first and, to date, only Hogwarts Express to be motor-powered. The train itself is the same design as set 4758 (see left), but is adapted to be motorized and comes with tracks, a power cord, a speed regulator, and a more elaborate version of Hogsmeade station.

First Hogwarts Express to come with rails

This Harry minifigure carries his black wand

Passenger windows now have clear transparent panes

New addition of a tender car

◄ Harry on the Hogwarts Express

This Harry minifigure appears only with the two 2004 Hogwarts Express sets.

HARRY POTTER (2004)

▼ Ron on the Hogwarts Express

This Ron minifigure comes with both of the 2004 train sets. His torso, with a stripy woolen sweater pattern, is not seen anywhere else. This expression is unique to Ron and comes on six of the ten Ron minifigures.

RON WEASLEY (2004)

DATA FILE

SET NAME: <u>Motorized Hogwarts Express</u>
YEAR: 2004   SET NUMBER: 10132
PIECES: 708   FILMS: III (POA)

COMPONENTS:
Locomotive engine; passenger car; Hogsmeade station building; motor; train tracks; frog; brown owl; white owl; rat; spider

MINIFIGURES:
4 (Harry Potter, Ron Weasley, Professor Lupin, Dementor)

coolest train

5972

cool

Train tracks form a circle

▼ Hogsmeade Station

This set builds on the Hogsmeade platform from set 4758 (see left). Rather than just a simple platform, the motorized train comes with a two-story model of the station building and a more elaborate platform.

HOGSMEADE STATION—BACK VIEW

HOGSMEADE

HOGSMEADE STATION—FRONT VIEW

POWER CORD

SPEED REGULATOR

Hogwarts Express (2010)

Roof lifts off

WHEN IT came to releasing the fourth Hogwarts Express set in 2010, LEGO® designers significantly developed the design of the train to further reflect the locomotive from the movies.

▼ Locomotive Engine

For the fourth locomotive, the LEGO Group created a new design. The result is this engine, with more detail and new stickers.

Engine room roof is smoother than previous design

Gold pieces were previously yellow

New gold element

▲ Passenger Car

This passenger car is a new design for 2010. Instead of compartments with benches, there are now backed seats with two walkways running the length of the carriage. It seats four minifigures with a table for each pair. Rather than splitting below the windows, the roof of this carriage can be removed to give easy access for playing.

HOGWARTS™ EXPRESS

5972

10

Fire grate slides in here

The back of the engine has a removable grate that clips out and can be filled with fuel from the coal car.

The removable grate for the fire is filled with black and transparent yellow pieces of coal.

New style of wheels

Clear lights are same as previous models

Magnet and sonar disks replaced with new parts

New snow plough

Glowing coal

FIRE GRATE

Coal Car

Previous Hogwarts Express sets had an engine and passenger car. 2010 saw the introduction of a coal car that is held magnetically between the engine and the carriage. It is topped with a single flat LEGO piece, whose studs create the impression of lumps of coal.

Under the layer of coal is a hidden luggage compartment. As well as suitcases, it has three small wand cases that are unique to this set.

Wand case

DATA FILE

SET NAME: Hogwarts Express
YEAR: 2010   SET NUMBER: 4841
PIECES: 646   FILMS: VI (H-BP)

COMPONENTS:
Locomotive engine; coal car; passenger car; Weasleys' flying car; food trolley; trunk; 3 owls; Invisibility Cloak

MINIFIGURES:
5 (Harry Potter, Ron Weasley, Ginny Weasley, Draco Malfoy, Luna Lovegood)

Chocolate Frog

Food Trolley

No trip on the Hogwarts Express would be complete without a treat from the food trolley. On one side, a sticker advertises Bertie Bott's Every-Flavor Beans. The other side includes a sticker that promotes Honeydukes sweet shop. Snacks include vanilla ice-cream and a Chocolate Frog.

All four minifigures have reversible heads

Freckles

Torso unique to this minifigure

New uniform design for 2010, with house badge and stripes

RON WEASLEY (2010)
Ron's two 2010 minifigures have a new tousled-style hair piece. In this set, Ron has two faces: scared and smiling.

GINNY WEASLEY (2010)
This minifigure of Ginny, unique to this set, looks older than her first one. Her double-sided head smiles and frowns.

DRACO MALFOY (2010)
Here, Draco's expression is troubled, but if you turn his head around, he is smirking. This minifigure is also unique to this set.

HARRY POTTER (2010)
Harry's torso is the same as in The Burrow (set 4840), but he has gray pants. One face smiles and one frowns.

The Knight Bus

OVER THE decades, LEGO designers have created a variety of transport—cars, buses, trains, ships, and airplanes—but this triple-decker, bright-purple bus is unique to LEGO Harry Potter.

▶ Triple-Decker Bus

This purple bus includes three levels for passengers with beds rather than seats, as well as plenty of room for luggage. The beds are designed to slide up and down with every bend in the road.

MAKE YOUR OWN

The instruction booklet gives alternative suggestions for the pieces of this set. Along the transport theme, there is a taxi and a more elaborate pick-up point.

Sirius Black's Animagus form

Lamppost

DATA FILE

SET NAME: Knight Bus

YEAR: 2004   SET NUMBER: 4755

PIECES: 243   FILMS: III (POA)

COMPONENTS:
Knight Bus; trunk; shrub; lamppost; dog (Sirius Black's Animagus form); Hedwig

MINIFIGURES:
2 (Harry Potter, Stan Shunpike)

Red bed sheets

Sloped tiles printed with pillow design

Shrunken head printed on windscreen

Minifigures enter via door at the back

Stan Shunpike

Wheels roll very easily

MINI SET

In 2004, the LEGO Group issued a promotional micro-scale version of the Knight Bus (set 4695). It was never available in shops, but came in limited promotions in movie theaters, with the LEGO® BrickMaster® Club, and with limited purchases of Hogwarts Castle (set 4757).

The solid model has no space inside and is not scaled for minifigures

The Mini Knight Bus, made of 58 bricks, is the only LEGO mini set to be released to date in the LEGO Harry Potter theme.

▶ Harry on the Knight Bus

This Harry minifigure, who is picked up by the Knight Bus after fleeing Privet Drive, is unique to this set. His torso pattern is not seen anywhere else and his wand comes with an extra attachment—a transparent cone that represents the *Lumos* spell.

HARRY POTTER (2004)

BRICK FACTS

What really makes this set special for LEGO fans is the inclusion of so many rare purple bricks. As well as their novelty value, they provide greater opportunities for MOCs ("My Own Creations").

▼ Stan Shunpike

Stan is the first LEGO minifigure ever to be made almost completely out of purple bricks.

Police hat piece in purple for first time

Conductor's ticket machine

Hair printed on face

STAN SHUNPIKE

EASY ACCESS

Layers between the floors are mostly covered with smooth tiles so the parts come apart easily for playability.

▼ Travel Accessories

There is plenty of space aboard the Knight Bus for luggage. Aside from his wand, Harry in this set also has a trunk, a bedding tile, and Hedwig. Other accessories in the set include a shrub, a lamppost, and a dog, which represents Sirius Black in his Animagus form.

Tile printed with bedding roll

Hogwarts Castle (2001)

HOGWARTS CASTLE, the home of Hogwarts School of Witchcraft and Wizardry, offered huge scope for LEGO designers' creativity. There have been four Hogwarts sets, released in 2001, 2004, 2007, and 2010.

► Interconnecting Towers

The first of the four Hogwarts castle sets is made up of a gatehouse and three towers. They can stand separately or be hinged together in any combination. There is the Great Hall, the Owlery, and Gryffindor Tower.

Transparent spell tile fits inside blue book

Poseable telescope for studying Astronomy

Box lid lifts up

Knight statue guards a jewel

Revolving entrance to Gryffindor common room

Stickered portrait of the Fat Lady

Lever pulls chain and opens box

Gryffindor common room

Scabbers, Ron's pet rat

Harry Potter climbing moveable stairs

◄ Crossing the Lake

Rubeus Hagrid accompanies first-years

Harry Potter

This set is based on the first movie, *Harry Potter and the Sorcerer's Stone.* It includes a molded rowing boat that Harry travels in across the lake to Hogwarts for the first time.

Chrome-effect key

Draco Malfoy

ROWBOAT

BRICK FACTS

Perhaps the most interesting of the library's many spell books are those in the Restricted Section. This one has a jacket with a howling, screaming face pattern.

Hinged book opens

↑ *2010 doesnt have that*

Draco Malfoy in tower

GATEHOUSE

GRYFFINDOR TOWER

Rocky outcrop

Restricted Section of library

Great Hall

Owlery Tower

Gryffindor
Tower

Gatehouse

▼ Peeves

The LEGO Group has created ghosts before, but never one using the standard minifigure pieces. This minifigure, made of gray bricks with faint, ghostly markings, is the mischievous poltergeist Peeves, who haunts the rooms of this Hogwarts set.

PEEVES (2001)

▲ Setting the Standard

This first LEGO Harry Potter castle set the style for all future Hogwarts releases. It introduced the roof tiles in sand-green, one of the LEGO's Group's special colors. The sand-green turrets have since become a trademark of LEGO Hogwarts architecture.

Plastic-laminated
paper roof

Double-sided
banner (Gryffindor
and Slytherin)

Ron Weasley on
the balcony

Crystal ball

Hinged chimney
breast reveals Peeves

Tower has
removable top

Owlery

Mezzanine level
for minifigures

DATA FILE

SET NAME: Hogwarts Castle

YEAR: 2001   SET NUMBER: 4709

PIECES: 682   FILMS: I (SS)

COMPONENTS:
Great Hall; Gryffindor Tower; Owlery Tower; gatehouse; rowboat; brown owl; gray owl; white owl; black owl; rat; bat

MINIFIGURES:
9 (Harry Potter, Hermione Granger, Ron Weasley, Draco Malfoy, Rubeus Hagrid, Professor Dumbledore, Professor Snape, Peeves, Knight statue)

Lion-shaped brick

Chair lifts up to reveal
secret compartment

GREAT HALL

**OWLERY
TOWER**

Letters delivered by owls

Glowing fire

Rotating fireplace

Professor Dumbledore

Hogwarts Castle (2004)

THE SECOND Hogwarts castle (set 4757) relates to events in the third movie, *Harry Potter and the Prisoner of Azkaban*. It continues the style of the first set, with sand-green, sand, and gray bricks, but has a new layout.

► Gryffindor Common Room

The Gryffindor common room can be accessed through a revolving door on the bottom level of Gryffindor Tower. In the first castle set, the entrance is decorated with a sticker of the portrait of the Fat Lady. However, because of an intruder in the third movie, she is missing from the picture here and the sticker is covered with tear marks.

MOTORIZED MECHANISM

This castle set incorporates a motorized LEGO® Technic mechanism with cogs that connect the clock face, a large pendulum, and the gearing that opens the Great Entrance doors. A lever on one side of the entrance causes the pendulum to rock, and a lever on the other side winds up the door grille.

Grille lifts so minifigures can enter castle

DOOR GRILLE

PENDULUM

COGS

Opening doors

CLOCK FACE

Whenever the motor is running, the clock face turns

▼ New Profile

Rather than a chain of towers, this castle set consists of three separate parts. The center piece is the main hall, which breaks apart into three separate sections. The rooms are full of surprises including moving parts and hidden compartments.

Central section breaks apart from two wings

Gryffindor Tower

Stained-glass window

Gryffindor shield

Two turrets open up

▼ Dementors at the Gates

Following events in *Harry Potter and the Prisoner of Azkaban*, the set introduces two LEGO Dementor minifigures.

Cloth cloak

Dementor minifigure

GATEHOUSE

DATA FILE

SET NAME: Hogwarts Castle

YEAR: 2004   **SET NUMBER:** 4757

PIECES: 944   **FILMS:** III (POA)

COMPONENTS:
Main Hall; Gryffindor Tower; gatehouse; black owl; white owl; 3 spiders; rat; frog; bat

MINIFIGURES:
9 (Harry Potter, Hermione Granger, Ron Weasley, Draco Malfoy, Professor Dumbledore, Professor Trelawney, 2 Dementors, white skeleton)

▼ Main Hall

The focal point of the new main hall is the Pendulum Hall with its Technic moving parts. The left-hand tower has a Potions classroom in the dungeon, a room for homework, and a trunk in the attic. The right-hand side has a dungeon, Professor Dumbledore's office in the middle, and Professor Trelawney's classroom in the turret. Also, look out for the small turret on the side that conceals a secret room.

BRICK FACTS

This potions brick is unique to LEGO Harry Potter and also appears in Snape's Class (set 4705) and Dumbledore's Office (set 4729).

▶ Gryffindor Tower

Gryffindor Tower has four stories for minifigures to explore, with the dormitory floor opening out for maximum playability. The entrance to the building is through the revolving door on the bottom level.

Sloped tile with potion and scroll printing

Crystal ball with skull inside

Professor Trelawney in her Divination classroom

Cups for reading tea leaves

Wings hinged to open out

Bed in each wing

Hidden room in turret has rotating blackboard with a skeleton behind it

Secret compartment in table

Dumbledore in his office

Revolving door

Ink bottle

Moving staircase

Pendulum

Potions classroom

Potions tile

MAIN HALL

GRYFFINDOR TOWER

Mandrake

To create the Mandrake plant, LEGO® designers combined old and new pieces. The magical plant is made up of a classic LEGO barrel and common three-leaved plant piece, together with a quirky new minifigure head.

Hogwarts Castle (2007)

THE THIRD release of Hogwarts Castle (set 5378) introduces new rooms and an all-new layout, based on the fifth movie, *Harry Potter and the Order of the Phoenix*.

Greenhouse

For the first time, Hogwarts castle comes with the greenhouse, where students study Herbology. When the room is closed, it is fully sealed, but hinges allow it to open to reveal the mysterious plants, a magnifying glass, and other studying aids.

Leaves sprout out of head

Screaming face printed on head

MANDRAKE

GREENHOUSE—OPEN

Blackboard with picture of Mandrake

Sand-green-colored LEGO piece

Transparent clear windows

Gaps below windows to ventilate plants

GREENHOUSE—CLOSED

Sand-colored LEGO piece

Vanishing Cabinet

Wall opens up to reveal entrance

Hinged for playability

Banners with Hogwarts school crest

The Room of Requirement

The Room of Requirement adapts itself to suit the needs of those who enter it, so this model has separate sections to reflect its varying uses. There is a large space at the bottom for Dumbledore's Army to practice their Defense against the Dark Arts, a room with the Vanishing Cabinet, and a room with seats and a table. The set comes with a spell target for students like Harry to practice their spells.

Turning piece makes target collapse

SPELL TARGET

ROOM OF REQUIREMENT

Draco Malfoy

DATA FILE

SET NAME: Hogwarts Castle
YEAR: 2007   **SET NUMBER:** 5378
PIECES: 943   **FILMS:** V (OOTP)

COMPONENTS:
Main castle; greenhouse; Room of Requirement; shooting range; 2 Thestrals; 2 Mandrakes; black owl; white owl; rat; bat

MINIFIGURES:
9 (Harry Potter, Hermione Granger, Ron Weasley, Draco Malfoy, Rubeus Hagrid, Professor Dumbledore, Professor Snape, Professor Umbridge, Death Eater (with black cloak)

► Hinged Towers

Rather than creating a chain of towers, this set is based around three hinged cubes: the main castle, which hinges open to reveal three towers, the Room of Requirement, and a greenhouse.

MAIN CASTLE

ROOM OF REQUIREMENT

◄ Main Castle

For playability, the main building splits into three hinged parts. On the bottom is the Gryffindor common room, the grand Entrance Hall, and the school library. The middle floor has a dormitory, the trophy room, and Professor Umbridge's office, complete with pink flowers, perfume bottles, and plates with kittens. The top floor houses the telescope for studying Astronomy.

Red book under the bed

Ron in the Astronomy turret

Angled tile with map of the constellations

Harry's confiscated Firebolt hidden in cupboard

Dumbledore in the trophy room

Pull down scroll to open cupboard doors

Ink quill

Professor Umbridge in her office

Restricted Section of library

Knight guarding hidden compartment

Professor Snape in the entrance hall

Tile with Sirius's head in fireplace

Trunk with Quidditch equipment

Crystal ball with a skull inside

31

Hogwarts Castle (2010)

FOR THE fourth Hogwarts set, the designer returned to the first movie to capture the classic profile of the castle. He was inspired by the first view of it as Harry crosses the lake. Rather than focusing on the latest movie, he also included elements from earlier movies, such as the library and Sirius Black, to give a sense of the castle through time.

▼ Common Rooms

Slytherin's common room is located at the bottom of this tower. Above it, a suit of armor stands guard beneath Gryffindor's common room. The tower is topped with an Owlery in the turret.

▼ Great Hall

Tables set for a feast are the focal point of the Great Hall, with its high ceiling and long, thin windows that capture the magic of the movies. The ceiling may not be enchanted to look like the night sky, but there is a rotating fixture of candles.

▼ Astronomy Tower

This tower houses the Room of Requirement, with its mysterious Vanishing Cabinet, the Restricted Section of the library, with its books of Dark Magic, and the Astronomy Tower.

Telescope swivels in any direction

Snape on Astronomy Tower

Gryffindor common room

Candelabra turns

Sirius Black's face appears in fireplace

Transparent bricks for stained-glass window

Suit of armor rotates

Gryffindor banner

Chairs swivel

Slytherin banner

Argus Filch

Mrs. Norris

Modular joining section

COMMON ROOMS

ASTRONOMY TOWER

Vanishing Cabinet

Harry Potter armed to defend Hogwarts

Slytherin common room

Room of Requirement

Hermione Granger at Gryffindor table

Set comes with six golden goblets

Two sloped tiles for Sorting Hat to sit on

Professor McGonagall at High Table

GREAT HALL

Professor Flitwick dressed for dinner

▼ Dumbledore's Office

The Hogwarts trophy room is at the base of the third tower. A rotating staircase leads up to Professor Dumbledore's two-story office which has many pieces to explore, including a Sorting Hat, the sword of Gryffindor, and two false-fronted cabinets that contain a letter and a Basilisk fang for destroying Horcruxes.

Sword of Gryffindor

Second LEGO Sorting Hat

DUMBLEDORE'S OFFICE

James Potter's Seeker trophy

Hidden compartment holds Basilisk fang

Moveable staircase

First Voldemort figure to come with a Hogwarts castle set

BOOKS UNDER LOCK AND KEY

Set 4842 revisits the idea of the Restricted Section of the library, but with a new advanced locking mechanism to keep out prying minifigures. Two keys release the chains (actually flexible hand-cuff pieces) so the clear panels of the cabinet can slide open.

▼ Modular Sections

The fourth LEGO castle returns to the design of the first in that it is made up of towers that fit together in a row. This set, however, introduces modular sections that give maximum flexibility by allowing the towers to be connected in any combination.

DATA FILE

SET NAME: Hogwarts Castle
YEAR: 2010   SET NUMBER: 4842
PIECES: 1290   FILMS: I–VII

COMPONENTS:
Great Hall; 3 towers; gray owl; brown owl; white owl; cat; 2 snakes; spider; bat; frog; rat; Sorting Hat; Marauder's Map; Sword of Gryffindor; Invisibility Cloak

MINIFIGURES:
11 (Harry Potter, Hermione Granger, Professor Dumbledore, Professor McGonagall, Professor Flitwick, Professor Snape, Argus Filch, Voldemort, 2 Dementors, Gryffindor Knight statue)

▼ Knight

This, the second version of the Knight minifigure, consists of a plain black head, gray torso, and gray legs, partly covered in armor pieces that have a special metallic finish.

Knight's closed helmet piece with eye slit

Pearl gray armor breastplate with protection for top of legs

Sword piece is shorter and less ornate than the sword of Gryffindor

GUARDED BY A KNIGHT

Below the Gryffindor common room, the Knight's statue hides a secret. He sits on a plinth that rotates to reveal Tom Riddle's diary slotted into the LEGO stonework.

VANISHING CABINET

The design for the LEGO Vanishing Cabinet has changed since it first appeared in 2007 in Hogwarts Castle (set 5378). The second design, which stands in the Room of Requirement in this set, is less ornate and has metal-colored bars and studs that make it look very secure.

This Vanishing Cabinet's partner is found in the Borgin and Burkes shop in Diagon Alley (set 10217)

VANISHING CABINET

Life at Hogwarts

MINIFIGURES BELONG to one of four houses at Hogwarts. Apart from sleeping, eating, and relaxing, there are numerous adventures to be had exploring the castle—but beware of Filch and his cat.

▼ Gryffindor Common Room

Minifigures belonging to Gryffindor house can relax in armchairs in this bright room that is part of Gryffindor House (set 4722). It comes with Ron Weasley, an owl, a rat, a transparent wand, and other supplies for a wizard school, all guarded by the Fat Lady.

Minifigures enter through rotating door

SET NAME	Gryffindor House	
YEAR	2001	NUMBER 4722
PIECES	68	FILMS I (SS)

Sticker of the Fat Lady also appears in Hogwarts Castle (set 4709)

GRYFFINDOR COMMON ROOM

Lamp made from an inverted radar dish piece

HARRY POTTER (2004)

The 2004 Gryffindor torso has a stripe and a colored tie but no school badge. Harry has a red lightning-shaped scar and he comes with Hogwarts Castle (set 4757).

RON WEASLEY (2004)

There are three versions of Ron in his uniform (2001, 2004, and 2010). This one has his common bowl-cut hair piece and is unique to Hogwarts Castle (set 4757).

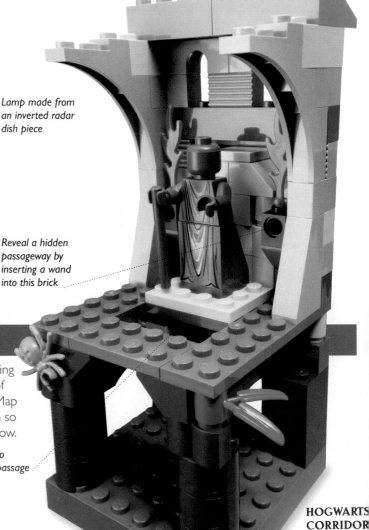

Reveal a hidden passageway by inserting a wand into this brick

Entranceway to underground passage

HOGWARTS CORRIDOR

▶ The Marauder's Map

Harry's minifigure should never be without the Marauder's Map if he is prowling the corridors of Hogwarts after lights-out. The tile piece shows the location of all the minifigures in the castle, and it comes with Harry and the Marauder's Map (set 4751). Inserting a wand into a Technic brick releases a locking mechanism so the statue's platform slides back, creating a passageway into the dungeons below.

SET NAME	Harry and the Marauder's Map	
YEAR	2004	NUMBER 4751
PIECES	109	FILMS III (POA)

MARAUDER'S MAP TILE

HERMIONE GRANGER (2001)

In Hogwarts Express (set 4708), Hermione does not know which house she will join, so her uniform shows the Hogwarts school badge. It is only later that her minifigures sport the Gryffindor crest.

NEVILLE LONGBOTTOM (2004)

Round-faced, buck-toothed Neville is captured in this minifigure with a cloak and black wand. He practices Defense Against the Dark Arts in Professor Lupin's Classroom (set 4752).

Skirt printed with hearts, stars, spots, birds, and horses

LUNA LOVEGOOD (2010)

Luna is a quirky Ravenclaw who comes with Hogwarts Express (set 4841). She has a skirt printed over her trousers and a double-sided head: One side with Spectrespecs and one without.

The Monster Book of Monsters

DRACO MALFOY (2004)

A Slytherin, Draco has a green stripe and tie on his uniform. This is one of four Draco minifigures in school robes and is from Draco's Encounter with Buckbeak (set 4750).

▶ The Sorting Hat

Hogwarts minifigures belong to Gryffindor, Slytherin, Ravenclaw, or Hufflepuff. This set, The Sorting Hat (set 4701), recreates the Sorting Ceremony that takes place at the beginning of every school year. Place a minifigure on the stool, with the hat on his or her head, and spin the wheel to select their school house.

SET NAME	The Sorting Hat	
YEAR	2001	NUMBER 4701
PIECES	48	FILMS 1 (SS)

◀ Caretaker

Argus Filch's minifigure walks the corridors of Hogwarts Castle (set 4842). He has the same hair piece as Dumbledore, but no beard; just stubble printed on his face.

ARGUS FILCH

Keys to go anywhere in Hogwarts

Tap piece used as handle of lamp

MRS. NORRIS

Three-stripe decoration is unique

Two yellow goblets

Minifigures can sit or stand

Tile scroll hidden in box

Harry has a general Hogwarts torso as he is not yet a member of Gryffindor house

Seat spins

Ravenclaw

Hufflepuff

Wand piece indicates selected house

SORTING CEREMONY

Gryffindor

SET NAME	Flying Lesson		
YEAR	2002	NUMBER	4711
PIECES	23	FILMS	1 (SS)

← smallest LHP set

2001 uniform torsos have house badges, striped v-necks, and colored ties

Brooms attach easily to minifigures' hands

DRACO MALFOY

HARRY POTTER

Remembrall has silver and gold detail

Draco Malfoy

WITH HIS trademark blond hair and smirk, Draco Malfoy is instantly recognizable in his eight different minifigure forms. Some are dressed for school, others show him in his Quidditch robes, and in one set he appears in black casual clothes while he shops in Quality Quidditch Supplies (set 4719).

▶ Slytherin Student

This Draco minifigure comes with Hogwarts Castle (set 5378) and shows him dressed for his studies in the Slytherin uniform with the 2004 torso. It is updated from Draco's 2001 minifigure (above) with a slightly more textured light-brown hair piece and a sneering face that replaces his original unfriendly expression.

BRICK FACTS

Neville Longbottom's Remembrall, unique to Flying Lesson (set 4711), is an example of the LEGO Group adapting existing pieces. It is a clear transparent minifigure head, decorated with gold and silver swirling details.

Green Slytherin colors on tie and sweater

DRACO MALFOY (2007)

▲ Potter vs. Malfoy

Drawn from the first movie, this scene from Flying Lesson (set 4711) recreates an early encounter between Draco Malfoy and Harry Potter. The set includes a unique piece for Neville Longbottom's Remembrall, which Harry tries to retrieve from Malfoy.

Slytherin play Quidditch in bright green

Slytherin badge

DRACO MALFOY (2004)

▲ Malfoy the Seeker

Draco's second Quidditch-playing minifigure has a flesh-colored rather than yellow face and hands, but the robes are the same—as is his trademark sneer. He is the only minifigure dressed for Quidditch in Hogwarts Castle (set 4757); his fellow students, Harry, Ron, and Hermione, are in their gray Gryffindor uniforms.

Two plant pieces each with six leaves

Buckbeak also comes with Sirius Black's Escape (set 4753)

Hippogriff model is half-horse and half-eagle

SET NAME	Draco's Encounter with Buckbeak	
YEAR 2004	NUMBER	4750
PIECES 36	FILMS III (POA)	

Hidden compartment

◄ Draco and Buckbeak

Draco appears in this scene that recreates one of Hagrid's Care of Magical Creatures lessons in which Draco encounters the Hippogriff Buckbeak (set 4750). The garden setting includes a hidden compartment in some rocks that contains a spider tile, feathers, and a tile printed with a bedding roll. The set also comes with an orange minifigure head posing as a pumpkin.

Flower stems with three large leaves

BUCKBEAK

DRACO MALFOY

▼ Slytherin House

The Slytherin common room is decorated with snakes and black, green, and gray LEGO® pieces. Draco's sidekicks, Goyle and Crabbe, each have dual-sided heads to represent Harry and Ron when they take Polyjuice Potion in *Harry Potter and the Chamber of Secrets*.

Wall section is hinged to open and close

Slytherin shield

Unique printed slimy pattern

HARRY POTTER AS GREGORY GOYLE

RON WEASLEY AS VINCENT CRABBE

Glass for Polyjuice Potion

Small potions table with a saucepan for a mini cauldron

SLYTHERIN COMMON ROOM

2001 uniform torso

SET NAME	Slytherin	
YEAR 2002	NUMBER	4735
PIECES 90	FILMS II (COS)	

Studying Magic

THE WORLD of LEGO® Harry Potter has many teachers, classrooms, spell books, wands, and other studying aids, all of which provide LEGO designers with scope to adapt existing pieces and create innovative new ones.

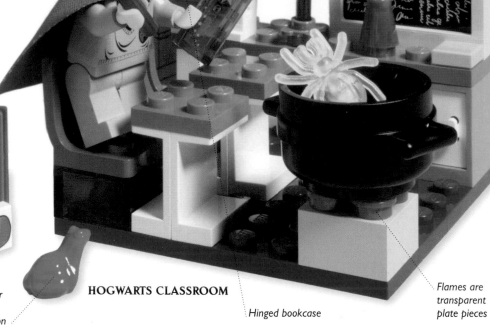

Window pane and frame pieces decorated to look like a blackboard

▶ Magical Classrooms

This scene is one half of Hogwarts Classrooms (set 4721). The other half is the scene with the Mirror of Erised (see page 11). Dressed in his uniform and a purple cloak, Harry brews potions in the Potions classroom.

SET NAME	Hogwarts Classrooms	
YEAR	2001	NUMBER 4721
PIECES	71	FILMS 1 (SS)

Frog for potion cauldron

HOGWARTS CLASSROOM

Hinged bookcase

Flames are transparent plate pieces

Witch's hat instead of hair piece

Glow-in-the-dark head

First Glow-in-the-dark minifig

Unique striped cloak

Flying goggles

PROFESSOR MCGONAGALL (2002)
The first Professor McGonagall minifigure appears in Dumbledore's Office (set 4729). Instead of poseable legs, she has a sloped brick that forms a long dress.

PROFESSOR MCGONAGALL (2010)
Professor McGonagall's second minifigure has a flesh-colored face, a stronger facial expression, and darker green robes in Hogwarts Castle (set 4842).

PROFESSOR SNAPE (2004)
Although this minifigure looks rather like Snape, it is actually a shape-shifting Boggart that has taken the Potions professor's form in Professor Lupin's Classroom (set 4752).

MADAM HOOCH (2002)
Flying instructor Madam Hooch's first minifigure has a flat-top hair piece. Her Quidditch robes include a Hogwarts shield to reflect her role as instructor in Quidditch Practice (set 4726).

Snake attached to back of rotating chair

▶ Disarming Charms

In this recreation of a scene from *Harry Potter and the Chamber of Secrets*, Harry and Draco's minifigures compete with each other in The Dueling Club (set 4733). The Technic mechanism in the dueling platform allows players to flip the minifigures as though they have been hit by a Disarming Charm.

Hogwarts banner showing all four houses

DUELING CLUB

Skull under glass dome

Professor Lupin

Lever to flip platforms

Barrel for storing wands

SET NAME	The Dueling Club	
YEAR	2002	NUMBER 4733
PIECES	129	FILMS II (COS)

◀ Defense Against the Dark Arts

Professor Lupin's Classroom (set 4752) recreates the moment when Neville Longbottom faces a Boggart who has taken the form of the thing he fears most: Professor Snape. Thanks to the Riddikulus Charm, the minifigure is dressed in Neville's grandmother's clothes.

SET NAME	Professor Lupin's Classroom	
YEAR	2004	NUMBER 4752
PIECES	156	FILMS III (POA)

PROFESSOR LUPIN'S CLASSROOM

Revolving cupboard door

Boggart as Professor Snape

Neville Longbottom

Hinged spider's web

Printed Magic Eye

Short, curled hair

Kitten brooch

Shawl

Silver buckles and straps

PROFESSOR FLITWICK (2010)

Professor Flitwick's short stature is reflected in his minifigure's short, unposeable legs. The Charms professor is unique to Hogwarts Castle (set 4842).

PROFESSOR TRELAWNEY (2004)

Professor Trelawney's minifigure has beads, bangles, and gauzy fabric printed on her torso. She works in the Astronomy Tower in Hogwarts Castle (set 4757).

ALASTOR "MAD-EYE" MOODY (2005)

Appearing in Harry and the Hungarian Horntail (set 4767), this minifigure of Mad-Eye Moody has the first non-brown pirate peg-leg used for a LEGO minifigure.

PROFESSOR UMBRIDGE (2007)

Professor Umbridge's minifigure is dressed in bright pink with a silk scarf and pretty brooch. She occupies a pink office in Hogwarts Castle (set 5378).

Professor Dumbledore

PROFESSOR DUMBLEDORE, the Headmaster of Hogwarts, is quite a distinctive LEGO® minifigure, with his long hair, beard, and the stern but kindly expression peering through his half-moon glasses. The LEGO Group has combined these elements in four Dumbledore minifigures and he has his own dedicated set: Dumbledore's Office (set 4729).

New eyebrow design

Printed silver embroidery

PROFESSOR DUMBLEDORE (2010)

One side of this head looks stern, the other smiles and does not wear glasses. It comes only with Hogwarts Castle (set 4842).

PROFESSOR DUMBLEDORE (2005)

The first sand-blue Dumbledore comes with Hogwarts Castle (set 5378) and Harry and the Hungarian Horntail (set 4767).

Wizarding gadgets

PROFESSOR DUMBLEDORE (2004)

This bright-purple-robed Dumbledore, which now has a flesh-colored face, is unique to Hogwarts Castle (set 4757).

Hair and beard now light bluish gray rather than dark gray

PROFESSOR DUMBLEDORE (2001)

The first Dumbledore minifigure, with purple wizarding robes, comes with this set, Hogwarts Castle (set 4709), and Hagrid's Hut (set 4707).

▶ Hidden Secrets

Here, Professor McGonagall's minifigure is investigating the three keys that hang on the wall of one of the lower-floor wings. Attached with small black claw pieces, each key slides out of the wall to reveal the unexpected: Tiles that are printed either as letters or with spells.

Black claw pieces grasp keys

▶ Middle Level

The middle floor has a secret hiding place in Dumbledore's desk for his letters. The wall panel behind it, which has a potion cabinet and a stained-glass window, also rotates to reveal a mystery key.

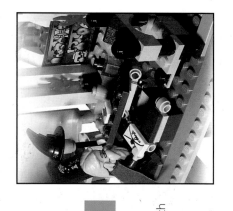

DATA FILE

SET NAME: Dumbledore's Office
YEAR: 2002   **SET NUMBER:** 4729
PIECES: 446   **FILMS:** II (COS)

COMPONENTS:
Three-story office; Sorting Hat; scorpion

MINIFIGURES:
3 (Professor Dumbledore, Harry Potter, Professor McGonagall)

Cogs make wheel spin and rotate wall panel below

Pattern swirls when disk spins

Headmaster's Office

Professor Dumbledore's office has a spiral staircase, moving parts, and secret compartments. It includes the Sorting Hat, potions, a key, and spell books.

Armchair swivels

Sorting Hat

Professor Dumbledore

16 pie-shaped pieces make up moving staircase

HARRY POTTER

One of two dragon wings

PROFESSOR McGONAGALL

Scorpion attached to key

DUMBLEDORE'S OFFICE—FRONT

Lever to make wheel spin

Secret entrance

DUMBLEDORE'S OFFICE —BACK

▲ Three Stories

Two floors of Dumbledore's Office close up into compact, closed boxes. Each has two wings that open up for accessibility. On the bottom floor, the doors open only when the mechanism under the dragon's head is unlocked using a scorpion key. There is another way in, however—the stained-glass window around the back lifts up to form a secret entrance.

Cool Office

Professor Snape

FACED WITH the task of creating a Snape LEGO® minifigure, the designers found a way to make this wizard stand out from the crowd—a glow-in-the-dark face. The Potions professor and Head of Slytherin house appears as five minifigures, which have special head pieces to capture his trademark scowl.

Furrowed brow

Silver decoration

PROFESSOR SNAPE (2010)

◀ Stern Professor

For Hogwarts Castle (set 4842) in 2010, Snape has a new facial expression with a crease between his eyebrows. His black locks are captured with a new tousled hair piece and he also has, for the first time, an all-black outfit,.

Sand-green roof pyramid is unique to LEGO Harry Potter

▶ Snape's Classroom

Set 4705 comes complete with a cauldron, shelves lined with colorful transparent jars for ingredients, and even its own poltergeist, Peeves.

SET NAME	Snape's Class	
YEAR 2001	NUMBER	4705
PIECES 163	FILMS	1 (SS)

PROFESSOR SNAPE

Panel beneath cauldron slides in to reveal a tile printed with a scroll pattern

Goblet for sampling potions

PROFESSOR SNAPE (2001)

The original Snape minifigure appears in Snape's Class (set 4705), Hogwarts Castle (set 4709), and The Dueling Club (set 4733).

Glow-in-the-dark head

PROFESSOR SNAPE (2004)

Here Snape has a similar outfit to his first minifigure, but with a slight difference in color and a cloak. He comes with Harry and the Marauder's Map (set 4751).

Printed hair

PROFESSOR SNAPE (2007)

This Snape minifigure has some of his hair printed on his face, as well as creases in his skin. He comes with Hogwarts Castle (set 5378).

BRICK FACTS

A gray version of this white piece is used in the LEGO Harry Potter set Dumbledore's Office (set 4729).

SET NAME	Professor Lupin's Classroom	
YEAR	2004	NUMBER 4752
PIECES	156	FILMS III (POA)

Head from skeleton minifigure

Plinth rotates

Key and frog hidden inside table

Peeves emerges from behind hinged cabinet

Potion ingredients

Defense Against the Dark Arts book

LUPIN'S CLASSROOM

SNAPE'S CLASSROOM

Working magnifying glass

RON WEASLEY

▲ Boggart as Snape

This minifigure is a shape-shifting Boggart that has assumed Snape's form because his teacher is the thing that Neville Longbottom fears the most. The minifigure emerges from Professor Lupin's Classroom (set 4752) on a rotating plinth that has a sticker of a wardrobe front on its reverse side.

Quidditch (2002)

THE LEGO Group has drawn from their experience in creating other sports sets to create two Quidditch LEGO® sets, released in 2002 and 2010.

Quidditch Practice (set 4726) is the LEGO Group's first recreation of Quidditch. The set comes with a tower for the referee, three goal posts, a catapult, and a trunk with the Quidditch balls, as well as three minifigures: Harry Potter, Draco Malfoy, and referee Madam Hooch.

SET NAME	Quidditch Practice	
YEAR	2002	NUMBER 4726
PIECES	128	FILMS II (COS)

As Seeker for the Gryffindor team, Harry is dressed in the red cloak and red-and-gold torso of Gryffindor's Quidditch robes.

Gryffindor badge

Golden Snitch attaches around a minifigure's hand, rather than being held in it

Gryffindor's Seeker

HARRY POTTER

HARRY POTTER (2002)

DRACO MALFOY

Slytherin's Seeker

Nimbus Two Thousand broomstick

Referee's chair

Hidden compartment under seat

Door opens up to reveal broom cupboard

LEGO Technic axles used for goal posts

DRACO MALFOY (2002)

Draco wears the green Slytherin Quidditch uniform. Silver detail on his torso highlights the markings on his Quidditch robes.

MADAM HOOCH

Catapult

The LEGO Group found a way to recreate the magic of Quidditch by bringing a LEGO element to the game. Players can use this to catapult fire balls into the air for LEGO playability.

Ball placed here

LEGO Technic pieces create hinge

TRU (TOYS "R" US) EVENT EXCLUSIVE

In 2002, the LEGO Group released a simplified, shorter tower for the Quidditch referee as a TRU Event Exclusive. Built out of blue and yellow bricks—the colors of Ravenclaw and Hufflepuff houses—the tower is a precursor to the tower produced in 2010 for Quidditch Match (set 4737).

Quidditch Kit

The Quidditch kit includes a red Quaffle, two black Bludgers, and the Golden Snitch.

Window pane also used for Honeydukes in Shrieking Shack (set 4756)

Shop's sign hangs from broomstick

LEGO flag piece holds Bludgers in place

Red Quaffle and black Bludgers are LEGO Technic ball joint pieces

Top of cloak stand piece is used in other LEGO Harry Potter sets for hand-held fiery torches

DRACO MALFOY (2003)

This minifigure of Quidditch player Draco has a yellow head and wears all black clothes. It is unique to Quality Quidditch Supplies (set 4719).

Barrel piece for flags, wands, and broomsticks

Quidditch through the Ages book with Quidditch designs

Quaffle

QUIDDITCH SHOP

Cash register unique to LEGO Harry Potter

Quality Quidditch Supplies

This set contains rare dark orange building pieces and comes with Draco Malfoy's minifigure.

SET NAME	Quality Quidditch Supplies	
YEAR	2003	NUMBER 4719
PIECES	120	FILMS II (COS)

That set is pointless

Have it ↓

Quidditch (2010)

THE LEGO® Quidditch sets are perfect for fans who want to recreate the fast-paced wizarding game. They come with lots of parts—minifigures on brooms, balls flung by catapults, and moveable goal posts—that can be played with in endless permutations.

◄ Flying Instructor

Madam Hooch's second minifigure comes with the second Quidditch set (set 4737) and has a double-sided head. One face wears a pair of detailed flying goggles and the other has large, yellow eyes.

MADAM HOOCH (2010)

Gray flying gloves

Gold detail on school badge and chain

ALTERNATIVE FACE

Golden Snitch

▼ Quidditch Match

For 2010, the LEGO Group revisited the theme of Quidditch and recreated a scene from the playing field. Quidditch Match (set 4737) has restyled goal posts, all-new Quidditch robes, and new features like the Quidditch Cup. It also includes two never-before-seen minifigures: Gryffindor's Captain Oliver Wood and Slytherin's Captain Marcus Flint.

Each goal hoop comes as a straight, flexible piece and is then bent into position

HARRY POTTER

Bludger

Beater's club

MARCUS FLINT

OLIVER WOOD

Catapult that fires balls in the set

DRACO MALFOY

Firebolt broomstick

DATA FILE

SET NAME: Quidditch Match
YEAR: 2010   **SET NUMBER:** 4737
PIECES: 153   **FILMS:** II (COS)

COMPONENTS:
Referee tower; three goal posts; trophy table; catapult; chest; 2 clubs; 5 broomsticks; 3 Bludgers; 2 Quaffles; Golden Snitch; Quidditch Cup

MINIFIGURES:
5 (Harry Potter, Oliver Wood, Draco Malfoy, Marcus Flint, Madam Hooch)

46

Gryffindor house badge

Madam Hooch watches the match from the referee's tower

Gryffindor Team

Team Captain Oliver Wood and Seeker Harry Potter represent the Gryffindor Quidditch team. Harry has a reversible head: When his team is winning, one side of his head smiles, but when it is losing, the other side frowns.

OLIVER WOOD

HARRY POTTER

Protective padding pattern

Slytherin Team

Slytherin Quidditch players are now dressed in darker green and have more detail on their clothing. Seeker Draco also has a new, slicked-back hair piece and a double-sided head. One side smirks and the other looks troubled.

Hands are brown to represent protective leather gloves

MARCUS FLINT

DRACO MALFOY

Red flag for Gryffindor

Green flag for Slytherin

BRICK FACTS

The minifigure-held club that the Beaters carry to hit the Bludgers at their opponents has actually been used in other LEGO sets, colored orange—as a carrot.

LEGO® Playability

The catapult in the 2010 Quidditch Match set is a smaller, simpler version of the one from 2002. However, it is just as effective at launching Bludgers into play on the LEGO Quidditch field.

Quidditch Cup is a new addition to Quidditch sets

LEGO Technic pivot

Archway tall enough for a minifigure to stand underneath

Metallic-effect trophy piece designed for 2010

Quidditch balls are LEGO Technic ball joint pieces

CATAPULT

Hagrid's Hut (2001–2004)

THE LEGO Group has released three versions of the popular set that is home to Hagrid—in 2001, 2004, and 2010. All three huts come with a range of LEGO® collectibles, which represent Hagrid's possessions.

Black rubber band

Chimney stack rotates to turn flames on and off in the fireplace

Paper roof pieces

Stone and moss effect

HUT (2001)—CLOSED

DATA FILE

SET NAME: Hagrid's Hut
YEAR: 2001   SET NUMBER: 4707
PIECES: 299   FILMS: 1 (SS)

COMPONENTS:
Eight-sided hut; cart; animal cage with a locking mechanism; Norbert the baby dragon; light-brown owl; spider; rat

MINIFIGURES:
2 (Rubeus Hagrid, Professor Dumbledore)

Wears brown gloves

Giant-sized belt buckle

Textured pocket

Door opens and closes

RUBEUS HAGRID (2001)

Hagrid is captured in three super-sized minifigures. This first one appears in set 4707, Gringotts Bank (set 4714), and Hogwarts Castle (set 4709).

▲ Stone Cabin (2001)

Hagrid's Hut, which is designed to sit alongside the first Hogwarts Castle (set 4709) in the school's grounds, hinges up to make a neat eight-sided box. The one-roomed cabin is a modest dwelling for Hagrid's oversized minifigure. A stone effect is created with gray bricks printed with stone and moss markings.

▶ Eight-Sided Hut

Creating an eight-sided hut on this scale proved an interesting challenge to LEGO designers. In order to construct a flexible, folding roof, they developed eight pieces of strengthened laminated paper. A black rubber band fastens around the studs at the top of the roof to hold the eight parts together.

Set includes two gold-effect keys

Eight floor pieces tessellate to cover floor when hut is closed together

Norbert the baby dragon sits in the fire

Hagrid's cart

HUT (2001)—OPEN

Hagrid's ax and pick-ax   _small_   **HAGRID**

Fireplace rotates

Fire grille is hinged

PROFESSOR DUMBLEDORE

Cupboard front opens to reveal book inside

HERMIONE GRANGER (2004)

In set 4754, Hagrid is visited by Hermione. Her minifigure has a magical Time-Turner printed on her 2004 Gryffindor torso.

like 2010 ✓

Time-Turner

A spider swings out when cupboard is opened

HUT (2004)—OPEN

Hidden compartment in fireplace hides a book

Different colored bricks now decorate walls

When opened out, hut creates patchwork floor

HERMIONE GRANGER

Mottled, chrome-brass key

RUBEUS HAGRID

DATA FILE

SET NAME: Hagrid's Hut
YEAR: 2004   SET NUMBER: 4754
PIECES: 302   FILMS: III (POA)

COMPONENTS:
Four-sided hut; bat; spider; rat

MINIFIGURES:
2 (Rubeus Hagrid, Hermione Granger)

▲ Four-Sided Hut

In 2004, the number of sides of Hagrid's hut was reduced from eight to four. This solved an engineering issue with the roof and meant that plastic bricks rather than paper could be used for the slanted sections. This represented a leap forward because the previous paper roof had been tricky for some young fans to assemble. Despite having only four walls, the hut is still packed with details and accessories, and it now has an extra doorway.

Sand-green tiles patch up roof

Sloped bricks create sense of ancient hut

New plastic roof

Pumpkin patch

HUT (2004)—CLOSED

▲ Stone Cabin (2004)

The new design for the sloped stone cabin swaps the dark-green roof trimmings for the sand-green pieces that are now an established mark of Hogwarts architecture in the LEGO sets. The new chimney stack section is assembled separately and then attached to the main hut with LEGO hinges.

▶ Rubeus Hagrid

Hagrid's second oversized minifigure has the same expression, but it now has flesh-colored hands and face. The printed robes are the same as those worn by the 2001 minifigure, but Hagrid now has moveable hands with three fingers on each one.

Hagrid is a minifigure head taller than a standard minifigure

Hidden compartment in chimney

Hagrid's crossbow

Giant-sized boots

RUBEUS HAGRID (2004)

Hagrid's Hut (2010)

THE THIRD release of this popular LEGO® model (set 4738) continues the architectural shape and style established in the previous Hagrid's Hut (set 4754), but introduces a new stone effect and more accessories. It also has more minifigures and an Acromantula, Aragog.

Hagrid's minifigur is too tall to walk upright through the door

Turkey leg splits in two

Unique owl

LIGHT-UP BRICKS

Little natural light finds its way into Hagrid's Hut so, for the first time, the would-be gloomy interior is illuminated by the fire in the hearth. An external button activates a battery-operated light-up brick in the fireplace.

Lever operates light-up fireplace

Key for Hogwarts

Fish hangs from rafter

Wrinkled face

New beard piece for Hagrid's minifigure

Glowing bricks in the fireplace

HUT (2010)—OPEN

◄ Rubeus Hagrid

Hagrid's new minifigure for 2010 has some small but distinctive modifications.

The structure of the minifigure is the same, but he has a new printed pattern for his brown robes. He also has new creases in the skin on his face.

Silver detail on belt buckle

Wizarding robes

RUBEUS HAGRID (2010)

Unposeable feet

▲ Hagrid's Revised Hut

Compared to the previous release of Hagrid's Hut, this new set has more brown—or wood-colored—bricks inside, which creates a more rustic, homely interior. Hagrid's home has giant-sized creature comforts, while tools and food hang from the rafters.

BRICK FACTS

In Hagrid's Hut (set 4738), Hagrid carries his "wand" disguised as an umbrella for the first time in LEGO Harry Potter. The "wand umbrella" is created in LEGO bricks by threading two pink cones onto a standard minifigure wand piece.

Hinged roof sections

Ax for chopping firewood

Hidden envelope

Stickered stone effect

Leaky, patched-up roof

HUT (2010)—CLOSED

Pumpkins are orange minifigure heads

▲ Stone Cabin (2010)

Like the previous Hagrid's Hut, set 4738 has four sides and a roof made of plastic bricks. However, instead of stones printed on the walls, this hut uses stickers with a pattern that highlights the edges of stones.

Table set for tea

New tousled hair piece for Ron

HARRY POTTER (2010)
Regular visitors to Hagrid's hut, Harry, Ron, and Hermione all come with this set. All three have double-sided heads so they can look happy or troubled.

RON WEASLEY (2010)
Gryffindor's uniform has undergone various redesigns. The 2010 torso combines both the house badge and the colored stripe across the bottom.

HERMIONE GRANGER (2010)
For 2010, these three minifigures all look a little older.

DATA FILE

SET NAME: Hagrid's Hut
YEAR: 2010   **SET NUMBER:** 4738
PIECES: 442   **FILMS:** VI (H-BP)

COMPONENTS:
Four-sided hut; Aragog the Acromantula; 3 spiders; Norbert the baby dragon; rat; brown owl; gray owl

MINIFIGURES:
4 (Rubeus Hagrid, Harry Potter, Hermione Granger, Ron Weasley)

Diagon Alley

OVER THE years, the shopping streets of Diagon Alley and Knockturn Alley have inspired several LEGO® models, including the 2003 Borgin and Burkes set. For 2011, the LEGO Group undertook a large-scale, ambitious project to create a sense of the bustling street, with Ollivanders and new Borgin and Burkes and Gringotts models.

2025! pieces?

UNPRECEDENTED DETAIL
2011 saw the first ever LEGO Harry Potter Direct Sale set. These are complex models designed exclusively for adult collectors and are available only from LEGO shops and LEGO.com.

AWESOME

Classic LEGO roof pieces used to create distinctive double-pointed roof

Potions

Wand cases

◀ Ollivanders

Minifigure wizards and witches buy their wands in Ollivanders. The simple two-sided LEGO building in blue, sand, and green bricks has ornate cast-iron-effect black trimmings and is full of details and decorations.

LEGO sextant piece used for light fitting

Fish in cauldron

Sign advertises cauldron sale

OLLIVANDERS—FRONT

Wanted poster

OLLIVANDERS—BACK

Moveable ladder for Mr. Ollivander to reach stock

Harry on the front page of The Quibbler

SET NAME	Diagon Alley	
YEAR	2011	NUMBER 10217
PIECES	2025	FILMS I–VII

MR. OLLIVANDER
Mr. Ollivander, the wandmaker, appears in this set for the first time as a LEGO minifigure. The wizard wears an old-fashioned neck-tie and vest, and his face has a creased brow and printed stubble.

◀ Borgin and Burkes (2003)

The dark colors of this early LEGO set from 2003 hint at the shop's connection to the Dark Arts. Borgin and Burkes is full of artifacts of Dark Magic, such as a minifigure brain, two printed eye pieces, two skulls, and the Hand of Glory tile. The chimney has a function that causes Harry's minifigure to fall into the shop through the Floo Network, as seen in the second Harry Potter movie.

SET NAME	Knockturn Alley	
YEAR 2003		NUMBER 4720
PIECES 209		FILMS II (COS)

Chimney contains Floo Network mechanism

BORGIN AND BURKES (2003)

HARRY POTTER

LUCIUS MALFOY

Minifigure head printed as a brain

Hand of Glory tile

Transparent black glass

Connection of flat windows creates rounded skylight-effect

▶ Borgin and Burkes (2011)

Diagon Alley (set 10217) has the second LEGO model of Borgin and Burkes. The dark, spooky shop now has a more detailed facade with a skeleton peering through the dusty window, and more features inside, including glow-in-the-dark bricks.

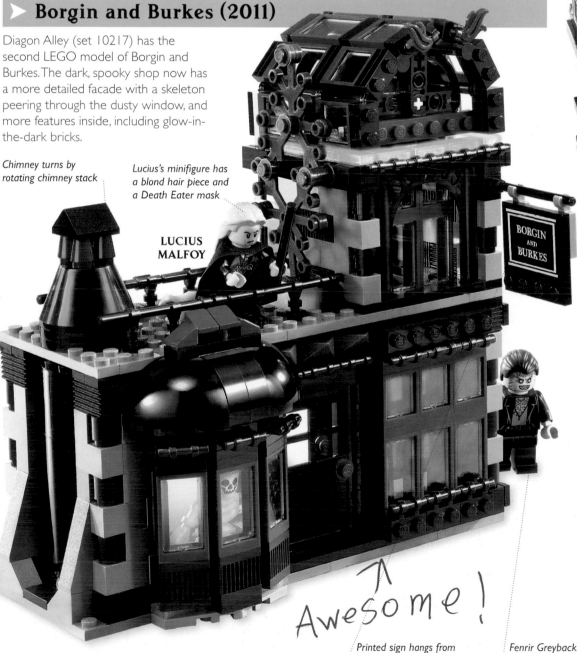

Chimney turns by rotating chimney stack

Lucius's minifigure has a blond hair piece and a Death Eater mask

LUCIUS MALFOY

BORGIN AND BURKES (2011)—BACK

▲ Dark Magic

As well as walking through the opening front door, minifigures can also enter the shop via the rotating chimney that is connected to the Floo Network.

SET NAME	Diagon Alley	
YEAR 2011		NUMBER 10217
PIECES 2025		FILMS I–VII

Awesome!

BORGIN AND BURKES (2011)—FRONT

Printed sign hangs from LEGO wand piece

Fenrir Greyback

BRICK FACTS

The LEGO Group has been making glow-in-the-dark bricks since a ghost piece in 1998, but they are rare. Borgin and Burkes contains several one-by-two glow-in-the-dark building bricks.

Gringotts

NOWHERE IS safer to store your LEGO® treasures than Gringotts, the wizard bank in Diagon Alley. LEGO designers have twice built the bank out of LEGO bricks: First in 2002 and then in 2011 as part of the Direct Sale set Diagon Alley (set 10217).

◀ Goblins (2002)

Gringotts is run by goblins, so in 2002 the LEGO Group turned its attention to creating the first ever goblin minifigures. Griphook and his colleague have specially molded heads with pointed ears and noses. They wear banking uniforms and, like Dobby the house-elf, they have short, non-poseable legs.

GOBLIN (2002)

GRIPHOOK (2002)

▶ Gringotts (2002)

The first Gringotts set comes in multiple parts and has great variety for playability. It consists of an entrance chamber with a removable counter and two safes, a bank vault, a trolley, a cart on rails, coins, money tiles, and a mysterious parcel that contains the Sorcerer's Stone. The set has four minifigures: Harry Potter in Muggle clothing, Hagrid, and two goblin bankers.

Section lifts out

Rotating safe

Trolley for transferring treasure to vaults

Hidden compartment under bat

Key fits into lock

Wizard money: Galleons, Knuts, and Sickles

Money tile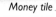

Minifigure can grasp handles

Rocky outcrop LEGO piece because vault is carved into rock

Harry's vault

BRICK FACTS

This tile, unique to LEGO Harry Potter, is printed with a magical scroll, cauldron, and goblet. As well as this set, it is in Chamber of Secrets (set 4730), Harry and the Marauder's Map (set 4751), Hogwarts Castle (set 4757), and The Dueling Club (set 4733).

Hagrid 2001 minifigure

"Gringotts" printed on LEGO brick

Harry Potter 2001 minifigure

Lever holds cart in place and sets it free

LEGO Technic axle piece

SET NAME	Gringotts Bank	
YEAR 2002		NUMBER 4714
PIECES 250		FILMS 1 (SS)

▲ Deep Underground

In order to reach the Gringotts bank vaults that are deep underground, the set comes with a cart and railtracks. The cart holds a goblin driver, Harry, and Hagrid standing on the back. A LEGO Technic mechanism has a lever that flips over and pushes the cart down the rails.

◄ Gringotts (2011)

As part of the 2011 Direct Sale Diagon Alley set, Gringotts has undergone a detailed overhaul. Its new imposing facade is closely matched to the styling of the movies with colored bricks to reflect white marble, burnished bronze, gold leaf, and aged wood.

SET NAME	Diagon Alley		
YEAR	2011	NUMBER	10217
PIECES	2025	FILMS	I–VII

BRICK FACTS

For the 2011 Diagon Alley set (set 10217), designers created three new owls—in gray, white, and brown—all printed with new details.

► Goblins (2011)

The two goblin minifigures who work in Gringotts have also been revised since 2002. The same head molds are now a white-skin color rather than cream. They wear the same uniform as each other, the torso of which is the same as Professor Flitwick's.

Wings of building fold in

GOBLIN (2010)

LEGO wand pieces make windows look secure

GRINGOTTS (2011)—FRONT (OPEN)

New LEGO piece for builders: a two-by-two round profile brick for ornate columns

Skylights are hinged to tilt up

LEGO graphic designers draw decorations like portraits

Large bank safe opens up

► Banking Hall

Stepping through the plastic wooden doors, minifigures find a large banking hall with a clerk's desk and large safe. The set does not have all of the components contained in the 2002 set, such as the cart, but, unlike that set, it has a substantial building, so the two sets complement each other well.

GRINGOTTS (2011)—BACK (OPEN)

Magical Creatures

THE MAGICAL creatures of LEGO® Harry Potter™ present challenges and opportunities to the LEGO creative team. Designers have found innovative ways to combine existing parts like a minifigure head or horse skeleton with new parts to bring these magical creatures to life in bricks.

Shelf tilts to drop bricks on troll

GIRLS' BATHROOM

Sink falls away from taps to mark entrance to Chamber of Secrets

▶ Mountain Troll

In Troll on the Loose (set 4712), based on *Harry Potter and the Sorcerer's Stone*, a large mountain troll roams around Hogwarts castle. The extremely large creature has a special minifigure head and its lumpy body comes as single piece, though one of its arms is articulated so that it can swing its club.

Bald minifigure head

SET NAME	Troll on the Loose	
YEAR	2002	NUMBER 4712
PIECES	71	FILMS 1 (SS)

Unique cloth clothes

Troll-sized club drags on floor

Elastic belt

Key turns in door

ALTERNATIVE BUILDS
Troll on the Loose has opportunities for turning the pieces into your own builds. Here is a suggestion from the instruction booklet where Harry escapes from a troll guard.

MOUNTAIN TROLL

Flat horned feet

HARRY POTTER

Harry fighting the troll

2002 Gryffindor torso

Thestral

The LEGO Group has not yet found a way to create bricks that are visible only to people who have experienced the death of a loved one, so these LEGO Thestrals can be seen by everyone.

Space for a minifigure to sit

Wings from dragon sets

Poseable head

SET NAME	Hogwarts Castle	
YEAR	2007	NUMBER 5378
PIECES	943	FILMS III (POA)

Body piece first created for a horse skeleton in the Castle theme

A Harry minifigure in development that has never been released

SET NAME	Sirius Black's Escape	
YEAR	2004	NUMBER 4753
PIECES	188	FILMS III (POA)

Wing pieces are used for Tom Riddle's grave in Graveyard Duel (set 4766)

Buckbeak

The Hippogriff called Buckbeak is made of three LEGO pieces: two wings and a unique body that is half-horse and half-eagle. He appears in Sirius Black's Escape (set 4753) and Draco's Encounter with Buckbeak (set 4750). Four studs on the Hippogriff's back enable a minifigure to be attached for a ride, either seated or standing up. Thanks to its articulated legs, a minifigure is able to bow to Buckbeak before approaching him.

Aragog

Whomping Willow

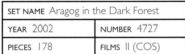

Aragog's home in the Forbidden Forest

SET NAME	Aragog in the Dark Forest	
YEAR	2002	NUMBER 4727
PIECES	178	FILMS II (COS)

Aragog's children

HARRY POTTER

RON WEASLEY

Abdomen is hinged

Hidden compartment in tree trunk

Lever makes spider webs flip over to trap minifigure

FORBIDDEN FOREST

Ron Weasley faces his biggest fear—spiders

Transparent red pieces behind eyes

Legs adapted from dinosaur pieces

ARAGOG (2002)

Pincers are horns from Viking helmets

BIONICLE® leg joints

Green stickered eyes

ARAGOG (2010)

The second Aragog is a more detailed design and has a printed face. It comes with Hagrid's Hut (set 4738), which is the site of Aragog's final resting place.

SET NAME	Hagrid's Hut	
YEAR	2010	NUMBER 4738
PIECES	442	FILMS VI (H-BP)

Blades from katana swords

Aragog, an Acromantula, has had two different LEGO bodies designed. The first has rubber legs and comes with Aragog in the Dark Forest (set 4727), which has her mechanical web, two spider children, terrified Ron and Harry minifigures, and the Whomping Willow. The scene is taken from *Harry Potter and the Chamber of Secrets* when Harry and Ron first meet Aragog in the Forbidden Forest.

Forbidden Corridor

IN THE first film, Harry, Ron, and Hermione complete a series of tasks to find the Sorcerer's Stone. These three tasks resulted in three sets: Forbidden Corridor (set 4706), The Chamber of the Winged Keys (set 4704), and The Final Challenge (set 4702).

Fluffy

Hinged trapdoor

▶ First Challenge

Forbidden Corridor is a perfect example of the LEGO Group's open building concept: Every part of the structure is easily accessible to maximize playability. The Sorcerer's Stone sets can be played with alone, or combined to recreate the series of chambers from the movie.

DEVIL'S SNARE
Falling through the trapdoor triggers branches of the deadly plant, Devil's Snare. Here, Ron has landed on the plant, causing another branch to fall on top of him. A red lever on the side releases the plant jaws.

Lever to release plant pieces

DATA FILE

SET NAME: Forbidden Corridor
YEAR: 2001   **SET NUMBER:** 4706
PIECES: 238   **FILMS:** 1 (SS)

COMPONENTS:
Forbidden Corridor; Fluffy; 2 spiders; 2 bats; flute

MINIFIGURES:
3 (Harry Potter, Hermione Granger, Ron Weasley)

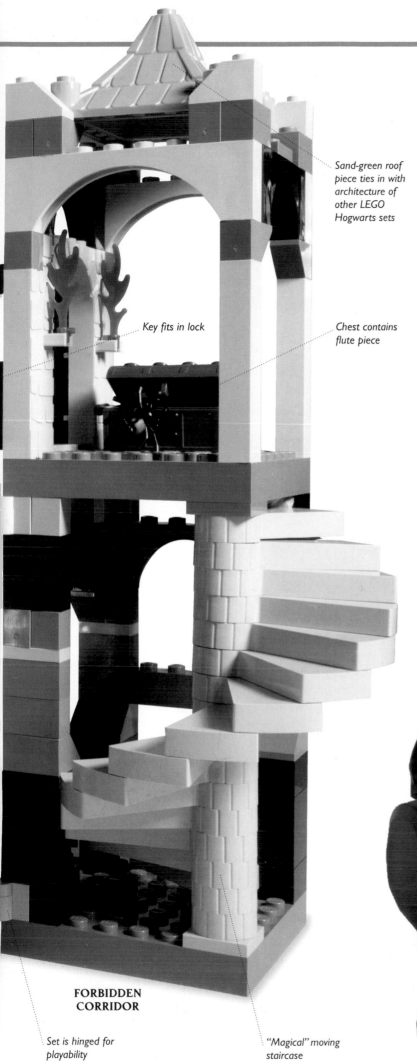

Sand-green roof piece ties in with architecture of other LEGO Hogwarts sets

Key fits in lock

Chest contains flute piece

FORBIDDEN CORRIDOR

Set is hinged for playability

"Magical" moving staircase

MAGICAL STAIRWAY

The LEGO Group captures some of the magic of the movies in many of their Hogwarts sets with their take on the castle's moving staircases.

16 pie-shaped pieces slot onto a central axis. Each step is attached only around the center, so each one can spin separately around the core.

The steps can spread out as a minifigure walks up or down them, until they are fully fanned.

▼ Fluffy

The Fluffy model is almost twice the size of a LEGO minifigure. This LEGO set also includes a flute, since the sound of music sends Fluffy to sleep.

Mouths open and close by moving head pieces

Black and brown parts come as one ready-assembled piece

Chamber of the Winged Keys

THIS SET, The Chamber of the Winged Keys, recreates Harry and Ron's attempts to complete the final two tasks to retrieve the Sorcerer's Stone.

▶ Challenges

With high ceilings and elegant arches, these two rooms look grand, but are simple to build. Topped with a Hogwarts-style sand-green turret roof, the model is true to the design of the castle it is a part of. The room on the left houses the chess board, and the room on the right is the chamber with the winged keys.

Door which the minifigures must unlock to move to next task

Chess Queen in middle of chess board

Small Chess Board

CHAMBER OF THE WINGED KEYS

2001 Gryffindor torso

RON WEASLEY

Nimbus Two Thousand

Chrome-effect shiny key with blue feathers

HARRY POTTER (2001)

◀ Flying Harry

In the Chamber of the Winged Keys, Harry's minifigure must identify the blue-winged key and use his broom skills to fly and catch it so he can unlock the door and progress to the next task. Harry's minifigure wears the 2001 Gryffindor uniform and a star-spangled cloak, and appears in eight LEGO Harry Potter sets from 2001 and 2002.

DATA FILE

SET NAME: The Chamber of the Winged Keys

YEAR: 2001   **SET NUMBER:** 4704

PIECES: 175   **FILMS:** 1 (SS)

COMPONENTS:
Chamber; spider; 4 gray keys; 2 shiny keys; broomstick

MINIFIGURES:
3 (Harry Potter, Ron Weasley, Chess Queen)

Space where brick has fallen from

Spider has a single stud, so it can attach to the center of the web

Hinged spider's web can fall down

Technic axle hole for holding key

◀ Chess Queen

The Chess Queen has a plain minifigure torso, a solid skirt piece with no poseable legs, and a blank face. Her head piece makes her appear more statue than human, as it is not the usual round minifigure head.

Brick falling from slot in wall

Chamber of Secrets

BASED ON the second movie, *Harry Potter and the Chamber of Secrets*, this set recreates the scene where Harry comes face-to-face with a Basilisk and Tom Riddle.

Serpent Gate

This piece of building, which forms the back wall of the Chamber of Secrets, is the portal through which the Basilisk emerges. As the serpent moves through, it pushes the double doors open.

Double-doors are on hinges

DATA FILE

SET NAME: Chamber of Secrets

YEAR: 2002 SET NUMBER: 4730

PIECES: 591 FILMS: II (COS)

COMPONENTS:
Chamber (in two parts); serpent's doorway; bathroom tower; Basilisk; Fawkes the phoenix; 5 snakes; gray owl; spider; Sword of Gryffindor; Sorting Hat

MINIFIGURES:
5 (Harry Potter, Ron Weasley, Ginny Weasley, Professor Lockhart, Tom Riddle)

Sword of Gryffindor hidden behind wall

Tom Riddle in Slytherin uniform

Face of Slytherin

Ginny Weasley

Basilisk

The Basilisk is made up of eight sand-green parts with darker green printed scales. Its fangs—which glow in the dark—are LEGO® pieces used as knives in other sets.

Knife pieces used for fangs—minifigures can hold them to destroy Horcruxes

Fangs glow in the dark

Two pieces hinge together to make long chamber

Stars on cloth cloak

Push in to flip open snake-panel doors

62

Established Hogwarts architecture pieces

▶ Professor Lockhart

This minifigure is one of only two made of Professor Lockhart. He wears a printed waistcoat with a cloaked suit in lilac.

Fawkes

Stained-glass window

Printed serpent pattern

Unique lilac cloak

PROFESSOR LOCKHART

Entrance to Chamber of Secrets through girls' bathroom

Push down to flip open trapdoor

Cool Basilisk

CHAMBER OF SECRETS

Tom Riddle's diary, stained with ink

▲ Deadly Chamber

The Chamber of Secrets model is made up of four parts: two long chamber walls, the Basilisk's entrance, and an entrance that is concealed in the tower with the girls' bathroom. All have unexpected moving parts.

Lever collapses snake-panel walls

Ron Weasley

Sirius Black

SIRIUS BLACK'S minifigure appears in Shrieking Shack (set 4756) and Sirius Black's Escape (set 4753). Sirius also appears in Animagus form in Knight Bus (set 4755), and as a face in the fireplace in Hogwarts Castle (set 5378).

SET NAME	Sirius Black's Escape	
YEAR	2004	NUMBER 4753
PIECES	188	FILMS III (POA)

Stone-molded wall pieces

Padlock piece attaches into key hole

◀ Escape from Azkaban

Sirius Black's minifigure has a stubbled face pattern, a long hair piece, torn clothes, and a torso printed with Azkaban prison attire.

Sirius is the only minifigure in Azkaban clothing

SIRIUS BLACK (2004)

Why is there a parrot?

▶ Sirius's Escape

Based on *Harry Potter and the Prisoner of Azkaban*, Sirius Black's Escape (set 4753) focuses around this Hogwarts prison tower. A small cell on the upper floor contains a bench, a goblet, and two torches. The tower opens up to reveal a second cell with hidden compartments. The set includes Sirius's minifigure, Buckbeak—who escapes with Sirius—and a Dementor.

Mouth pursed to give Dementor's Kiss

▲ Animagus

As an Animagus, Sirius Black can take the form of a dog. His molded LEGO dog piece appears in Knight Bus (set 4755) and Shrieking Shack (set 4756).

DEMENTOR

HOGWARTS PRISON TOWER

Rat-infested cell

Tile slides in and out of fireplace

◀ Face in the Fire

Although Sirius's minifigure only comes in two LEGO sets, his face appears on a tile in Hogwarts Castle (set 5378). The tile represents when he uses Floo powder for a clandestine conversation with Harry in the fireplace of the Gryffindor common room.

SET NAME	Hogwarts Castle	
YEAR	2007	NUMBER 5378
PIECES	943	FILMS V (OOTP)

Harry's black wand

Buckbeak and Harry Potter both come with Sirius Black's Escape (set 4753)

HARRY POTTER

Molded feather detail

SIRIUS BLACK

LEGO crenellated castle wall

Potion bottle with jewel stopper

Wings flap up and down

BUCKBEAK

Buckbeak is a Hippogriff

Lid lifts up to reveal black key inside

Whole unit hinges forward with hidden compartment underneath

Hair printed around top of head to show bald patch

Werewolf scratches on face

Torn pattern on suit

PETER "WORMTAIL" PETTIGREW (2004)

Peter "Wormtail" Pettigrew comes with Sirius in Shrieking Shack (set 4756). In Graveyard Duel (set 4766), Peter has the same torso, but has a hair piece and more whiskers.

PROFESSOR LUPIN (2004)

Lupin's minifigure comes with Hogwarts Express (set 4758), Motorized Hogwarts Express (set 10132), and Professor Lupin's Classroom (set 4752).

The Shrieking Shack

INSPIRED BY the village of Hogsmeade, designers at the LEGO Group created three buildings for this set, number 4756: the Shrieking Shack, Honeydukes candy store, and the Transfiguration shed.

Roof rotates up and over

Bed tilts, tipping minifigures to floor below

Secret entrance behind chimney

Turn to tilt bed

SHRIEKING SHACK—BACK

Peter Pettigrew

Hidden compartment in table

PROFESSOR LUPIN

Printed scratches on face

HOLD TIGHT!

Minifigures should be careful in the Shrieking Shack: Danger lurks in unexpected places. Taking a seat on the bed could see a minifigure plunging to the floor below: Turning the lever outside the window tilts the bed through the floor.

◀ Werewolf

Professor Lupin's usual minifigure (from Professor Lupin's Classroom (set 4752), Hogwarts Express (set 4758), and Motorized Hogwarts Express (set 10132)) is seen here, but with an additional head piece for when he becomes a werewolf.

PROFESSOR LUPIN/ WEREWOLF

▶ Harry in Hogsmeade

This minifigure is unique to this set. Harry is in casual clothes when he goes to the Shrieking Shack. His torso, with a brown T-shirt and gray open shirt, also comes with the *Harry Potter and the Prisoner of Azkaban* train set releases (sets 4758 and 10132), but here he wears light-brown rather than blue pants.

HARRY POTTER (2004)

▲ Haunted Building

LEGO® designers recreated the Shrieking Shack's scary look from the films, and just as in the movie, there is more to the building than it first appears: There are moving parts, a hidden compartment, and a secret entrance.

Snow-capped windows

Printed wood-grain effect

Doors and windows boarded up

SHRIEKING SHACK—FRONT

Whole house rotates 360°

That is cool

▲ Creaking Building

Boarded up windows and gloomy, dusty colors recreate the creepy atmosphere of this dilapidated old house. To add to this effect, there is a turntable piece between the cellar and the ground floor that makes the upper house wobble and creak.

Button to switch between chambers

◁ Transfiguration Shed

LEGO Animagi can switch between their human and animal forms in this shed. Place the shed over one model and press the button. Lift the shed up, and the original model has disappeared! It has been replaced by the other model!

Shed contains two chambers

Set has two Animagi: Sirius Black and his dog form and Peter Pettigrew and his rat form

HUMAN FORM

DOG FORM

INSPIRING BUILDERS
The instruction booklet for this set encourages fans to create their own makes with other ideas for the pieces in this set, including these three small buildings and a fence panel using the wood-grain panels.

▼ Honeydukes

Inside, Honeydukes contains many LEGO goodies, like popsicles, cherries, and tiles of chocolate. A sloped roof-tile, printed with a cash register pattern, is ready and waiting for the pocket money of Hogwarts students on a visit to Hogsmeade.

HONEYDUKES—BACK

Camouflaged trapdoor

Shop is hinged for playability

Cash register

Popsicles advertise candy store

Sirius Black in Azkaban outfit

Inviting shop display

Panes printed with leading and jars

HONEYDUKES—FRONT

Durmstrang Ship

THE LEGO Group has created a vast array of sets with nautical themes. In developing LEGO Harry Potter, LEGO designers took their LEGO shipbuilding skills a step further. The result is this magnificent Durmstrang Ship.

▽ Igor Karkaroff

Igor Karkaroff, the headmaster of the Durmstrang Institute, has a torso printed with a shaggy, matted fur cloak with toggles, and a large hat piece.

▽ Removable Cabin

The closed cabin on the upper deck lifts off for easy playability and opens up to reveal a cozy room for reading, writing, and relaxing on long journeys. The room below has open doorways, so this is the only place for minifigures to hide away from rough waves and sea storms.

▽ Below Deck

Under the removable cabin is a room only accessible by taking off the cabin and the upper deck that forms this room's roof. Also hidden away is a secret compartment. The table-top lifts up to reveal tools, including a rare LEGO sextant piece.

IGOR KARKAROFF (2005)

BRICK FACTS

This special tile, printed with a handwritten scroll with two spindles, appears on board this ship and in Hogwarts Castle (set 5378).

Quill pen and ink pot

CABIN

Magnifying glass and tile printed with scroll of parchment

Barrel for crow's nest is scaled for minifigures.

▶ Durmstrang Ship

The ship is 53 cm (20⅞ in) tall and 51 cm (20 in) long. There are three levels of decking and two cabins to explore, but minifigures should beware of being flipped overboard by the moveable plank.

Crane for loading cargo

Cloth flags in Durmstrang colors

DATA FILE

SET NAME: The Durmstrang Ship
YEAR: 2005   SET NUMBER: 4768
PIECES: 550   FILMS: IV (GOF)

COMPONENTS:
Ship with detachable room; bat

MINIFIGURES:
2 (Igor Karkaroff, Viktor Krum)

From The Tournament

▶ Viktor Krum

Viktor Krum's minifigure has the same printed body and hat as Igor Karkaroff. Krum's minifigure, however, looks younger thanks to his lack of mustache and less fierce expression, which makes it easy to distinguish between the two Durmstrang minifigures.

VIKTOR KRUM (2005)

Simple Bottom

Ship's wheel

Old-fashioned nautical map

Pearl-finished gold window lattice

Viktor Krum

Hull is made from two specially molded pieces

Removable cabin

TARGET EXCLUSIVE

2005 saw an exclusive version of this set for the Target store with bonus minifigures: Harry and Dumbledore from the Hungarian Horntail (set 4767) and Hermione and Ron from Rescue from the Merpeople (set 4762).

Igor Karkaroff

Deck lifts off

Black Falcon shield

Durmstrang Stag shield

Small chrome gold bolts sparkle

Pressing plank launches minifigures overboard

The Hungarian Horntail

THIS IS a recreation in bricks from the movie *Harry Potter and the Goblet of Fire*. It shows Harry's first task in the Triwizard Tournament.

Cool outfit

Harry's Firebolt broomstick

"POTTER" repeated in large letters on back of torso piece

◀ Golden Egg

Here, Harry poses with the golden egg he retrieves to pass the first task. This shiny gold ball posed a problem for LEGO® designers. How could they get Harry to hold something spherical? They solved this problem in a brand new way: By creating a small handle that fits perfectly into a minifigure's hand and attaches magnetically to the ball.

Manetic Attach

HARRY POTTER (2005)

◀ Triwizard Harry

This Harry minifigure has his tousled hair piece and a flesh-colored head with a red lightning-shaped scar, but the torso is unique. He is dressed in his Triwizard champion uniform. The first task he faces is not easy, so the printed pattern on his shirt shows tattered and ripped fabric.

HARRY POTTER (2005)

Catapult delivers Harry's broomstick to him

Pearlized magnetic ball is unique to this set

Rocky outcrop forms dragon's enclosure

BRICK FACTS

The transparent fiery-colored pieces used for the dragon's fire-breath are used throughout LEGO Harry Potter in different guises. As well as flames for flambeaux and hand-held torches, they appear in transparent blue for water and transparent green for seaweed.

▼ In the Arena

In this set, the Hungarian Horntail dragon is tethered in an enclosure formed by LEGO rocks, with the golden egg nestled in the middle. However, the LEGO dragon can get loose from its chains. The spectators also face a second threat: If the LEGO chain is pulled, the two tiers of viewing seats flip, flinging them into the air.

ARENA

▶ Hungarian Horntail

The Hungarian Horntail has a newly designed body, head, and barbed tail. Its wings are a classic shape, but have new duo-tone shaded coloring.

Awesome Dragon

Printed vertical pupils

Transparent neon-orange fire-breath

DATA FILE

SET NAME: Harry and the Hungarian Horntail

YEAR: 2005   **SET NUMBER:** 4767

PIECES: 265   **FILMS:** IV (GOF)

COMPONENTS:
Hungarian Horntail dragon; enclosure; golden egg; spectator stand; bat

MINIFIGURES:
3 (Harry Potter, Professor Dumbledore, Mad-Eye Moody)

Hogwarts school crest

Durmstrang school crest

Beauxbatons school crest

Mad-Eye Moody

Only set that he is in

Professor Dumbledore

Collapsible viewing stand

Chain tethers dragon—until it breaks free

Pot for the golden egg

71

The Lake

RESCUE FROM the Merpeople (set 4762) is based on the fourth movie, *Harry Potter and the Goblet of Fire*. It recreates the scene of the second task in the Triwizard Tournament.

◀ Viktor Krum

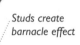

VIKTOR KRUM (2005)

This human minifigure with a shark's head is the second version of Viktor Krum. It reveals how the Durmstrang champion partly Transfigures himself so he can swim deep into the lake. The minifigure also comes with a human head piece with black hair.

That's weird

▼ Merperson

The design of this Merperson is brand new for the LEGO Harry Potter range, and has unique coloring and patterns. Thanks to her extra-high tail piece, she stands a head taller than human minifigures.

Hair piece is same shape as Dumbledore's

MERPERSON

▼ Watery Prison

Ron and Hermione's minifigures are submerged deep in the lake near Hogwarts castle, and guarded by a Merperson. The set has a mechanical function that shoots them up into the air.

Archway with stone effect appears in other LEGO Harry Potter sets in bluish-gray, light gray, light-brown, and orange

Frame tilts back

Studs create barnacle effect

Flame-shaped pieces used for seaweed

Lever (behind Hermione) flings minifigures into air

Two knives hidden within step

Crab

Swimming trunks

MERPEOPLE'S VILLAGE

Viktor's Durmstrang champion uniform

◄ Enchanted

Hermione and Ron's faces show them sleeping as they are magically enchanted while they await rescue. However, their heads are double-sided, so when they are rescued, their faces can return to their normal expression.

ALTERNATIVE FACE

**HERMIONE GRANGER
(2005)**

**RON WEASLEY
(2005)**

Freaky Faces

Fits three minifigures

Rotatable oarheads

Hull can be extended with additional pieces

▲ Rowboat

Unlike the rowboat that Hagrid and the first-years use to cross the lake in Hogwarts Castle (set 4709), this shallow LEGO boat is made up of multiple pieces and has moveable oars.

► Lobster

To add to the theme of life on the lake bed, this set includes a rock cave, made out of four different shades of blue bricks. When pushed from behind, it shoots a lobster across the room.

Element fires lobster out of cave

Who Cares? **CAVE**

BRICK FACTS

This scorpion piece appears in many LEGO guises. In this set, it is a red lobster. A transparent neon-orange scorpion is for sale in Diagon Alley Shops (set 4723), and a dark gray one is part of a locking mechanism in Dumbledore's Office (set 4729).

Stud for attaching another piece

▼ Gillyweed Harry

This unique Harry minifigure shows the effects of Gillyweed. One side of Harry's head is printed with gills for breathing underwater and he has flippers at the end of his usual feet. For the first time in LEGO bricks, the hip piece is a different color to show swimming trunks.

Printed gills

"POTTER" printed on torso back

Removable flippers

HARRY POTTER (2005)

FLYING TO FREEDOM

Hermione and Ron's minifigures, held captive in the lake, are standing on two long LEGO pieces that slide into the platform. When a lever at the back of the arch is pushed, a shooting mechanism flings the minifigures into the air—and to freedom.

LEGO poles slide into base

Voldemort

WHEN LEGO® Harry Potter™ began in 2001, He Who Must Not Be Named had no physical form. As Voldemort's strength has returned, however, the LEGO designers have come up with different ways to represent him.

Glow-in-the-dark head

◄ New Body

In his first corporeal form, Voldemort's minifigure from Graveyard Duel (set 4766) has a Dementor-style cloak and a serpentine face pattern.

VOLDEMORT (2005)

Bald head

Snakelike nose slits

White LEGO wand

▼ Professor Quirrell

With The Final Challenge (set 4702), LEGO Harry Potter introduced the first ever double-sided head. Professor Quirrell's purple turban can be removed to reveal Voldemort's face. The double-sided head has since become widely used across all LEGO themes.

Door revolves and reveals the Sorcerer's Stone jewel piece on its other side

SET NAME	The Final Challenge	
YEAR	2001	NUMBER 4702
PIECES	60	FILMS 1 (SS)

Lenticular sticker flickers between Harry with and without the Sorcerer's Stone

Sorcerer's Stone is a red LEGO jewel that fits in a minifigure's hand

HOGWARTS

Serpentine eyes, nose, and mouth

ALTERNATIVE FACE

PROFESSOR QUIRRELL (2001)

One side of Professor Quirrell's face has an ordinary yellow minifigure expression. The other side has Voldemort's evil features.

VOLDEMORT (2010)

DEVELOPMENT PROCESS

Creating LEGO sets is a constant process of revision and refinement. At one point, the Voldemort minifigure for the 2010 Hogwarts Castle (set 4842), wore green rather than his final black outfit, though the patterns on his torso remained.

Metal hand

WORMTAIL (2005)

Peter "Wormtail" Pettigrew, from Graveyard Duel (set 4766), has whiskery facial markings to indicate that his Animagus form is a rat.

Dapper suit under cloak · *Lucius's hair piece*

DEATH EATER (2005)

The other side of this Death Eater's head reveals Lucius Malfoy's face. He appears in Graveyard Duel (set 4766).

DEATH EATER (2007)

This anonymous Death Eater is from Hogwarts Castle (set 5378). The mask is printed with silver detail.

BELLATRIX LESTRANGE (2010)

An ornate silver and blue outfit and a unique hair piece make Bellatrix, from The Burrow (set 4840), distinctive.

Hairy, wolflike face

FENRIR GREYBACK (2010)

Werewolf Fenrir's minifigure has a face with vicious-looking markings. He causes trouble in The Burrow (set 4840).

◀ Voldemort (2010)

For 2010, LEGO designers were able to design a more human-looking Voldemort minifigure. His head and hands are deathly white and his facial pattern is somewhere between his original snakelike features and a regular minifigure. He is one of very few minifigures to have any markings for a nose. He is dressed all in black with some green detail.

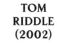

TOM RIDDLE (2002)

◀ Tom Riddle

Voldemort was once an ordinary Hogwarts school boy called Tom Riddle. Tom's LEGO minifigure appears in Chamber of Secrets (set 4730). Tom wears a Slytherin uniform, human expression and black cloak. He also has the same hair piece as Harry Potter's minifigure.

2002 Slytherin torso with house badge

Screaming mouth and hollow cheeks are their only facial features

DEMENTOR (2004)

DEMENTOR (2010)

◀ Dementors

The Dementor minifigures are an ingenious collection of LEGO pieces that make them far from human. Under their raggedy cloth cloaks they have skeleton torsos and, instead of legs, they stand on a single pole. Two Dementor LEGO minifigures have been released. The first, in sand green and gray, was replaced for 2010 with a gray and black design.

Graveyard Duel

GRAVEYARD DUEL (set 4766) is based on the scene in the movie *Harry Potter and the Goblet of Fire* when Harry witnesses the return of Lord Voldemort.

This unique Harry minifigure is dressed in his Triwizard champion uniform.

HARRY POTTER (2005)

Cover is made up of two pieces that separate

Skeleton pops up when handle is turned

GRAVES
Dark secrets lurk in all four graves, but this one is the most elaborate.

Removable roof for playability

WHITE SKELETON

This white skeleton has five standard pieces, but its evil skull pattern makes it rare.

BLACK SKELETON

The black version of the white skeleton— with the evil skull pattern—is unique to this set.

BLACK-AND-GREEN SKELETON

These sand-green chest and arms pieces are the same as those used under Dementors' cloaks.

False floor lifts up to reveal skeletons

Grave-digging tools

Skull-shaped tombstone

Hinged coffin contains half-dug up skeleton legs

Brick printed with half-dug up skeleton torso

HARRY POTTER

BRICK *FACTS*

Two of the graves contain tiles printed with partially disturbed skeletons. Matching the two tiles together creates one whole skeleton.

GRAVEYARD

▼ Graveyard at Little Hangleton

Rather than one focal building, Graveyard Duel is a a grouping of elements: a crypt, tree, cauldron, hearse, four graves, and seven minifigures, all framed by padlocked railings. The graves are different designs, but they all hold macabre surprises.

Four black bats and two black owls

Building arch pieces make curved branches

DATA FILE

SET NAME: Graveyard Duel

YEAR: 2005   SET NUMBER: 4766

PIECES: 548   FILMS: IV (GOF)

COMPONENTS:
Tom Riddle's grave; 3 other graves; cauldron; crypt; spooky tree; railings; hearse; 4 bats; 2 black owls; bird; frog; 3 snakes

MINIFIGURES:
7 (Harry Potter, Voldemort, Wormtail, Death Eater, white skeleton, black skeleton, black-and-green skeleton)

Tom Riddle's grave lifts up to reveal snake pit

Skeleton attached to tree

Wagon has removable coffin piece

TOM RIDDLE

Sacrificial knife

PETER "WORMTAIL" PETTIGREW

Cauldron for potion to bring back Voldemort

DEATH EATER

Death Eater resembles Lucius Malfoy

Lance handle opens grave

VOLDEMORT

Padlocked chain allows just enough room for minifigures to squeeze through

Beyond The Brick

Behind the Scenes

Henrik leads the creative team.

HENRIK SAABY Clausen is the design manager of the LEGO® Harry Potter™ team in Billund, Denmark. He has worked at the LEGO Group for 15 years and has been involved with LEGO Harry Potter since its inception in 2000. DK met with Henrik and the rest of his team to find out how the magic happens.

Originally, the LEGO Group was given this model of Harry Potter for reference based on the artwork from the books. However, reference material from the films was used to create the first LEGO sets.

WHO ARE THE LEGO HARRY POTTER TEAM?

The team who worked on the 2010 and 2011 sets (below) brought knowledge from previous Harry Potter projects as well as from other themes, for example Hans Henrik Sidenius, who designed the latest Hogwarts Express, began his LEGO career working on trains. Everyone is very enthusiastic and passionate about their work, and also in the detail and the quality of the sets they produce.

HOW IS THE TEAM ARRANGED?

Every creative team at the LEGO Group contains a mix of roles, who work under the direction of a design manager like Henrik. Designers come up with the ideas and visualization of the sets. Graphic designers visualize all the two-dimensional printed designs, such as newspaper tiles, stone-effect patterns, and minifigures' expressions and clothes. Part designers are engineers who take the designers' ideas and, with their help, turn them into moldable, functioning pieces that fit with the LEGO system. Part designers also make molds for test models of all the new parts. A project supporter keeps everything on track, and keeps a

Element drawers contain all the LEGO pieces that are currently in production, such as these minifigure parts.

record of all the bricks and colors being used, so no-one uses too many new pieces. The design manager, who has responsibility for the schedule and budget, oversees the team and liaises with engineering, production, and marketing.

HOW DOES A PROJECT BEGIN?

The starting point for any new release is knowing how many sets will be done, what their price points are, and how many new pieces can be used. Also the size of a set is important to know. For 2011, Nicholas Groves designed our first ever LEGO Harry Potter Direct Sale set (Diagon Alley, set 10217). These large-scale, complex sets are a fun opportunity for designers, but also pose challenges. Once we have this starting point, some designers sketch their ideas in pencil; others prefer to use computer-aided design software like Rhino.

WHAT DETERMINES WHETHER A PIECE IS PRINTED OR STICKERED?

Graphic designers Chris Bonven Johansen and Martin Fink share the design of these details. As creative lead, Henrik pushes for printed elements rather than stickers wherever possible. Printed bricks are easier to play with and they give a sense of quality.

The Harry Potter design team in 2010. Back, left to right: Henrik Saaby Clausen (design manager), Chris Bonven Johansen (senior graphic designer), Bjarke Lykke Madsen (senior designer), Nicholas Groves (designer), Sven Robin Kahl (designer). Front, left to right: Luis F. E. Castaneda (designer), Gitte Thorsen (senior designer and sculptor), Hans Henrik Sidenius (designer), Martin Fink (graphic designer).

RON'S ROOM
GINNY'S ROOM
OPEN BACK
BRIDGE
MR · MRS WEASLEY BEDROOM
STAIRS
STAIRS
MAIN HOUSE
FRONT
HALF DOOR
KITCHEN / DINER

The words on this development sketch are in English. Although the LEGO Group is a Danish company based in Billund, Denmark, they have a large number of international staff and English is their official language of business.

WHAT ARE YOUR INFLUENCES?

We use the movies, the books, and the Harry Potter computer games for inspiration, along with other reference material from Warner Bros. When new movies are being made, we visit the movie sets, read the scripts, and study the artwork. Designers love to include small elements as a nod to the props in the movies, for example Luis F. E. Castaneda added the pig in its sty to The Burrow (set 4840). Sometimes we also combine key moments from a location into one set: Sven Robin Kahl included Aragog into the 2010 release of Hagrid's Hut (set 4738) to give a sense of action and to differentiate it from the previous Hagrid's Hut sets. We also have a consumer service that gives us feedback from fans about what new things they would like to see, which we try to work into our models.

WHAT IS THE NEXT STEP IN THE PROCESS?

Models go through several evolutions of development before they are ready; four is average. Sometimes it's a case of refining elements so they can be physically molded into LEGO bricks; sometimes it's a case of reducing the number of new elements involved. The first design of the 2010 Hogwarts Castle (set 4842) was very close to its final version. Senior designer Bjarke Lykke Madsen was inspired by the scene in the first movie where the castle is seen, across the lake, for the very first time. He faithfully reproduced this profile, which he saw as the strongest representation of the castle, and which proved successful in capturing an iconic shape that needed little revision.

WHAT KIND OF TESTS DO THE SETS GO THROUGH?

We have an internal Model Committee that puts every LEGO set through a rigorous process. Each person builds the set by following the instructions to make sure that it works and that the age marking is correct. They also ensure

2010 LEGO Color palette:

Solid:
24 106 21 221 23 · 28 119 192 18 01 26 · Effects: 131
226 · 222 212 · 37 · 05 283 208 · 297
191 · 124 102 135 151 · 138 38 194 · 148
154 268 140 · 141 · 312 · 199 · 294
308

Transparent:
44 182 47 41 113 126 42 43 143 48 311 49 111 40

Rather than using the standard Pantone System for color referencing, the LEGO Group has its own internal system, based on the exact nature of the plastics and inks that they use. There are around 50 colors to choose from. "151" is the sand-green used in Hogwarts sets and "05" is sand, also very common in LEGO Harry Potter.

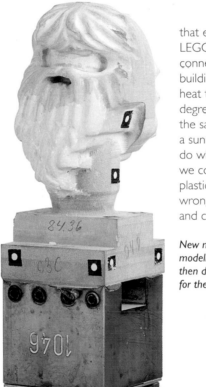

that everything is consistent with the LEGO system: That every element can connect to every other to give maximum building possibilities. Sets also go through heat testing. Putting them in an oven at 60 degrees Celsius for four hours simulates the same conditions for plastic as sitting on a sunny windowsill for a long time. We also do what we call the "butter test" where we cover them in butter. Butter does good plastic no harm, but if there is something wrong with the plastic, then it will tarnish and crack! We also have arrangements

New minifigure pieces are hand-sculpted in modeling clay at a ratio of 1:3. This prototype is then digitally scanned. From this image, the mold for the plastic pieces is made.

with local schools and their children come to the LEGO Group every Wednesday to try out new sets. Sometimes we watch them playing to see how they react, and sometimes they take things home and then answer questions about them.

All bricks are produced in metal molds. Senior designer and sculptor Gitte Thorsen took great care to ensure that every angle of Bellatrix's complex, curly hair is removable from the metal casing.

Going Digital

have it for Wii ↓

THE COMPUTER game LEGO® *Harry Potter™: Years 1–4* blends the creativity of LEGO bricks with the rich characters and storytelling of Harry Potter to create a colorful and exciting digital environment. Made by TT Games, the game is an opportunity for players to become their favorite character and explore their magical world.

▼ LEGO® *Harry Potter™: Years 1–4*

The game charts Harry's first four years at Hogwarts with "cutscenes"—which retell the stories from a fresh LEGO perspective—and gameplay, where you use spells to complete tasks and unlock new levels. It is available on a wide variety of different devices, including PSP, Xbox 360, PlayStation 3, Nintendo Wii, PC, and Nintendo DS. There are also versions for iPhone and iPad.

PSP GAME PACKAGING

As well as animating all the existing well-loved LEGO minifigures, the game also introduces new characters that have yet to be realized in physical LEGO bricks, such as Harry's cousin Dudley.

DUDLEY DURSLEY

XBOX 360 GAME PACKAGING

Characters are the heart and soul of LEGO® Harry Potter™: Years 1–4. Players can take control of 170 characters, from Hermione, Ron, and Harry to Draco Malfoy or even He Who Must Not Be Named.

HERMIONE GRANGER

RON WEASLEY

HARRY POTTER

Harry's abilities include Expecto patronum for fending off Dementors. He can also use his Invisibility Cloak

Ron's rat Scabbers helps in tasks by crawling through small pipes

Hermione's Time-Turner ability allows players to time travel

Hermione's cat Crookshanks has the ability to dig

Magical Gameplay

By moving through the game completing lessons and adventures, you learn spells that help you complete tasks. One such spell is *Wingardium Leviosa* that allows you to lift objects—and even other characters. As you learn new skills, you also trigger new areas of Hogwarts and progress through the storyline.

PROFESSOR LOCKHART

LEGO characters are brought to life by exaggerating their personalities, which also adds humor to the game.

Clothing matches LEGO minifigure, but personality is added through movement

Abilities

As well as knowledge, which you gather as you go, players can use the innate talents of their characters. Multiple players can also work together as different characters to complete tasks. Harry is excellent at flying, but don't call on Hermione for a broom task! However, she is useful when it comes to figuring out tricky puzzles or deciphering symbols.

PROFESSOR DUMBLEDORE

As players progress, new characters are unlocked. You need to work hard to unlock a character as powerful as Professor Dumbledore.

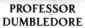

Making the Digital World

TT GAMES brought its experience of making many LEGO® computer games to creating its first ever LEGO Harry Potter game. A team of 80 people, including coders, artists, animators, designers, production, audio, and quality assurance testers, worked for almost two years to produce the ground-breaking game.

Fully poseable animation of Draco Malfoy

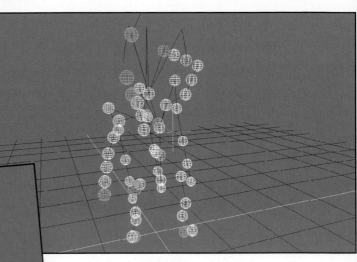

STEP ONE

◄ Bringing Characters to Life

LEGO minifigures capture a wealth of detail, but translating them into an animated world of movement creates new opportunities for expressing personality. TT Games designers have a lot of fun creating individual personalities, though it can be a challenge to get the maximum expression while staying true to the LEGO styling. In the animation rig for Draco Malfoy (above), each sphere indicates a moveable part. Draco is then mapped onto this rig, allowing the animators to manipulate him into a full range of poses (left).

Mad-Eye has his own special animation rig because of his peg leg and false eye. It also allows him to drink from a potion bottle.

MAD-EYE MOODY

STEP TWO

BUILDING A DIGITAL WORLD

The world of LEGO Harry Potter is brought to life in an extensive 3-D environment, where players can explore their favorite locations from Diagon Alley to Hogwarts Castle. These three images show the progress from the initial mapping of a level to the finished article. Step one shows the basic environment geometry. Step two shows the same scene, but with polished puzzles and finishing art applied to the geometry. Step three shows the final scene, now perfectly lit and with all the effects applied.

Gray areas show where computer-controlled characters are able to walk

STEP ONE

Scenes from the main intro from The Prisoner of Azkaban

THE PRISONER OF AZKABAN
MAIN INTRO

Shot 42
The bus screeches to a halt in front of cam. Harry is thrown up against the glass.

Shot 43
Slo Mo cam. the bus rolls forward.

Shot 44
The driver pulls down a lever as the cam. pans around him.

Shot 44
Slo Mo cam. The lego bricks break apart as the bus squeezes through.

© Copyright Traveller's Tales (UK) Ltd. 2008

LEGO bricks of the Knight Bus come apart as it squeezes between buses

THE PRISONER OF AZKABAN
MAIN INTRO

Shot 45
Harry stretches as the bricks break apart around him.

Shot 46
Slo mo cam. as the bus comes out and bricks re-assemble.

Cam. normal speed kicks in as the bus zips o.s.

Shot 47
The bus swerves around the traffic as it crosses the bridge.

Shot 48
Cam. pans down from roof top of the leaky cauldron.

Continue pan down past neon sighn.

THE PRISONER OF AZKABAN
MAIN INTRO

pan pauses as a traffic warden writes out a ticket for broom stick.

Cam. pans across as the Knight Bus rounds the corner.

Shot 49
Bus screeches to a stop outside the leaky cauldron.

Shot 50
The driver waves to the traffic warden.

Shot 51
The warden angrily writes out a ticket.

© Copyright Traveller's Tales (UK) Ltd. 2008

◄ Storytelling

Storyboards map out cutscenes before animation. Cutscenes retell the story in a condensed format, so a 20-minute section from the film might be cut down to 90 seconds. This makes things snappy while keeping the important story points. The storyboards are very close to the final scenes, but occasionally animators may make changes as they're creating them. For example, when Harry takes the egg to Moaning Myrtle in Year 4, the storyboards showed her simply indicating where Harry should go next. However, because Myrtle is a fun and distinctive character, the animator added some extra color and humor. Now Myrtle attracts Harry's attention to the exit by performing a synchronized swimming routine.

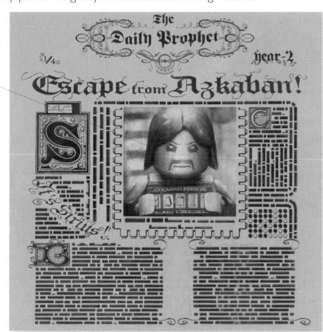

Sirius Black's escape from Azkaban is front-page news

Neon sign of the Leaky Cauldron pub

▲ Attention to Detail

The game is filled with props, such as this *Daily Prophet* article about Sirius Black, which are painstakingly designed to be accurate to the movie, while keeping their unique LEGO style. Artists use detailed reference materials, as well as the movies, to create recognizable art and props so that objects and places create a believable and realistic game world.

Angry traffic warden writes the Knight Bus a ticket

STEP TWO

STEP THREE

Merchandise

THERE'S MORE to LEGO® Harry Potter™ than LEGO bricks and sets to build and play with. You can play the computer games, challenge your friends with the board game, decorate your fridge with magnets, and keep track of your keys with minifigure key chains.

▼ Hogwarts Board Game

In keeping with the LEGO ethos, there is no right or wrong way to play this board game from the LEGO Group's board game team. Using creativity and imagination, you can determine the building of the board's 332 pieces, the gameplay, and even the rules, as you go.

This is fun →

Ravenclaw common room

Divination classroom

Microfigure moves around board

Homework items

Slytherin common room

The six-sided die has one dot, two dots, and three dots to move as many staircases; two sides with a brown symbol to rotate a staircase; and one side with the Marauder's Map to use a secret passage.

Brown staircase pieces

Transfiguration classroom

Potions classroom

RON WEASLEY

HARRY POTTER

PROFESSOR DUMBLEDORE

HERMIONE GRANGER

DRACO MALFOY

The game comes with microfigures of five LEGO Harry Potter characters that can be used for more alternative gameplay.

Each player chooses a house and moves their microfigure around the board via the brown staircase pieces that can be moved according to the throw of the die. The winner is the first to get back to their common room having collected the four homework pieces in their house color from each of the classrooms. The game includes lots of additional gameplay—as well as suggesting you create your own rules.

◀ Creator Computer Game

In 1998, the LEGO Group began its Creator series of computer games, in which players build locations out of virtual LEGO bricks and complete tasks. The first LEGO Harry Potter Creator game was released in 2001. A second, based on the second movie, soon followed.

Creator game is developed by the company Superscape and published by Electronic Arts (EA)

The first game is based on the first movie, Harry Potter and the Sorcerer's Stone

Library

Hufflepuff common room

Players can only enter rooms via the arched doorways

▲ Minifigure Magnets

The minifigure magnets include Harry, Professor Snape, and Draco minifigures or a set containing Harry dressed for Quidditch, Professor Dumbledore, and Hermione. The magnets are designed by the Extended Line team, an in-house department at the LEGO Group.

▶ Minifigure Key Chains

These LEGO Harry Potter key chains first appeared in 2004. The in-house LEGO Group Extended Line team created them from existing minifigures, in liaison with the LEGO Harry Potter team.

2006   **2007**   **2010**

2004

Spaces for homework items

Gryffindor common room

Sand-green turret pieces reflect Hogwarts architecture in sets

All characters are the same size as standard minifigures

 2010   **2010**   **2010**   **2010**   **2010**

2011 Releases

IN 2011 the LEGO Group introduced four sets: A large-scale Diagon Alley (10217) pictured on pages 52–53 launched on January 1st, 2011 and three more sets released in June 2011—The Forbidden Forest (4865), The Knight Bus (4866), and Hogwarts (4867).

The Knight Bus

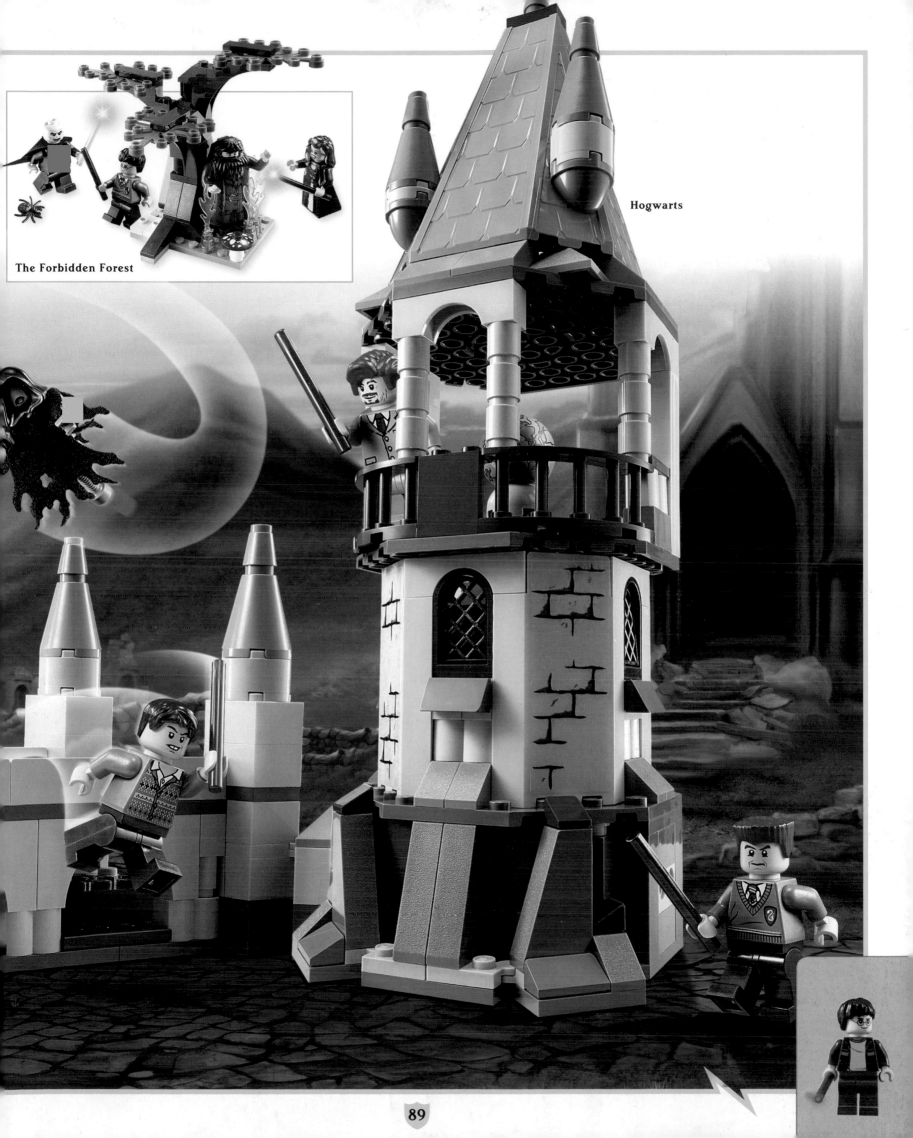

The Forbidden Forest

Hogwarts

Minifigures

THE LEGO® minifigure has come a long way since the first one in 1978, and LEGO Harry Potter has introduced new characters, expressions, and techniques, such as the first glow-in-the-dark head. Exactly four LEGO bricks high without a hat, minifigures come in three basic parts—a head; torso (with arms and hands); and hips and legs—plus many have hair pieces and accessories like a wizard's cloak or wand.

HARRY POTTER (2001)

Sets: 4708 • 4714

See page 18

HARRY POTTER (2002)

Set: 4728

See page 10

HARRY POTTER (2002)

Set: 4727

See page 57

HARRY POTTER (2003)

Set: 4720

See page 53

HARRY POTTER (2004)

Set: 4755

See page 66

HARRY POTTER (2004)

Sets: 4758 • 10132

See page 21

HARRY POTTER (2004)

Set: 4755

See page 25

HARRY POTTER (2010)

Set: 4840

See page 14

HARRY POTTER (2010)

Set: 4841

See page 23

HARRY POTTER (2001)

Sets: 4702 • 4704 • 4711 • 4712 • 4729 • 4730 • 4733

See page 10

HARRY POTTER (2001)

Set: 4701

See page 10

HARRY POTTER (2001)

Sets: 4706 • 4709 • 4721

See page 11

HARRY POTTER (2004)

Set: 4751

See page 11

In 2003, the LEGO Group switched from yellow to flesh-colored skin for all licensed properties, including LEGO Harry Potter

HARRY POTTER (2004)

Set: 4753

See page 11

HARRY POTTER (2007)

Set: 5378

See page 11

HARRY POTTER (2010)

Sets: 4736 • 4738 • 4842

See page 51

HARRY POTTER (2002)

Set: 4726

See page 44

HARRY POTTER (2010)

Set: 4737

See page 47

HARRY POTTER (2005)

Set: 4762

See page 73

HARRY POTTER (2004)

Set: 4757

See page 34

HARRY POTTER (2005)

Set: 4766

See page 76

HARRY POTTER (2005)

Set: 4767

See page 70

HARRY POTTER (2011)

Exclusive to this book.

See page 11

VERNON DURSLEY (2002)

Set: 4728

See page 10

HERMIONE GRANGER (2001)

Set: 4723

See page 16

HERMIONE GRANGER (2011)

Set: 10217

HERMIONE GRANGER (2001)
Sets: 4706 • 4709
See page 16

HERMIONE GRANGER (2001)
Set: 4708
See pages 35, 49

HERMIONE GRANGER (2004)
Set: 4757
See page 16

HERMIONE GRANGER (2004)
Set: 4754
See page 49

HERMIONE GRANGER (2005)
Set: 4762
See page 73

HERMIONE GRANGER (2007)
Set: 5378
See page 16

HERMIONE GRANGER (2010)
Sets: 4738 • 4842
See page 51

RON WEASLEY (2001)
Sets: 4708 • 4728
See pages 12, 19

RON WEASLEY (2001)
Set: 4722
See pages 19, 34

RON WEASLEY (2002)
Set: 4727
See page 57

RON WEASLEY (2004)
Sets: 4758 • 10132
See page 21

RON WEASLEY (2010)
Set: 4841
See page 23

RON WEASLEY (2011)
Set: 10217

RON WEASLEY (2001)
Set: 4704 • 4705 • 4706 • 4709 • 4730
See page 13

RON WEASLEY (2004)
Set: 4757
See page 34

RON WEASLEY (2005)
Sets: 4762 • 5378
See pages 12, 73

RON WEASLEY (2010)
Set: 4738
See page 51

GINNY WEASLEY (2002)
Set: 4730
See page 13

GINNY WEASLEY (2010)
Set: 4841
See page 23

GINNY WEASLEY (2010)
Set: 4840
See page 13

FRED WEASLEY (2011)
Set: 10217
See page 13

GEORGE WEASLEY (2011)
Set: 10217
See page 13

MOLLY WEASLEY (2010)
Set: 4840
See page 13

ARTHUR WEASLEY (2011)
Set: 4840
See page 13

NEVILLE LONGBOTTOM (2004)
Set: 4752
See page 35

LUNA LOVEGOOD (2010)
Set: 4841
See page 35

OLIVER WOOD (2010)
Set: 4737
See page 47

DRACO MALFOY (2003)
Set: 4719
See page 45

DRACO MALFOY (2001)
Sets: 4709 • 4711 • 4733 • 4735
See page 36

DRACO MALFOY (2004)
Set: 4750
See page 35

DRACO MALFOY (2007)
Set: 5378
See page 36

DRACO MALFOY (2010)
Set: 4841
See page 23

DRACO MALFOY (2002)
Set: 4726
See page 44

DRACO MALFOY (2004)
Set: 4757
See page 36

DRACO MALFOY (2010)
Set: 4737
See page 47

MARCUS FLINT (2010)	**GREGORY GOYLE** (2002)	**VINCENT CRABBE** (2002)	**LUCIUS MALFOY** (2002)	**LUCIUS MALFOY** (2003)	**LUCIUS MALFOY** (2010)	**PROFESSOR DUMBLEDORE** (2001)	**PROFESSOR DUMBLEDORE** (2004)	**PROFESSOR DUMBLEDORE** (2005)
Set: 4737	Set: 4735	Set: 4735	Set: 4731	Set: 4720	Set: 4736	Sets: 4701 • 4709 • 4729	Set: 4757	Sets: 4767 • 5378
See page 47	See page 37	See page 37	See page 17	See page 53	See page 17	See page 40	See page 40	See page 40

PROFESSOR DUMBLEDORE (2010)	**RUBEUS HAGRID** (2001)	**RUBEUS HAGRID** (2004)	**RUBEUS HAGRID** (2010)	**PROFESSOR QUIRRELL** (2001)	**PROFESSOR SNAPE** (2001)	**PROFESSOR SNAPE** (2004)	**PROFESSOR SNAPE** (2004)	**PROFESSOR SNAPE** (2007)
Set: 4842	Sets: 4707 • 4709 • 4714	Sets: 4754 • 5378	Set: 4738	Set: 4702	Sets: 4705 • 4709 • 4733	Set: 4751	Set: 4752	Set: 5378
See page 40	See page 48	See page 49	See page 50	See page 74	See page 43	See page 43	See page 38	See page 43

PROFESSOR SNAPE (2010)	**PROFESSOR MCGONAGALL** (2002)	**PROFESSOR MCGONAGALL** (2010)	**MADAM HOOCH** (2002)	**MADAM HOOCH** (2010)	**PROFESSOR LOCKHART** (2002)	**PROFESSOR LOCKHART** (2002)	**PROFESSOR TRELAWNEY** (2004)	**"MAD-EYE" MOODY** (2005)
Set: 4842	Set: 4729	Set: 4842	Set: 4726	Set: 4737	Set: 4733	Set: 4730	Set: 4757	Set: 4767
See page 42	See page 38	See page 38	See page 38	See page 46	See page 39	See page 63	See page 39	See page 39

PROFESSOR UMBRIDGE (2007)	**PROFESSOR LUPIN** (2004)	**PROFESSOR LUPIN** (2004)	**PROFESSOR FLITWICK** (2010)	**ARGUS FILCH** (2010)	**SIRIUS BLACK** (2004)	**PETER PETTIGREW** (2004)	**PETER "WORMTAIL" PETTIGREW** (2005)
Set: 5378	Sets: 4752 • 4758 • 10132	Set: 4756	Set: 4842	Set: 4842	Sets: 4753 • 4756	Set: 4756	Set: 4766
See page 39	See page 65	See page 66	See page 39	See page 35	See page 64	See page 65	See page 75

STAN SHUNPIKE (2004)
Set: 4755
See page 25

MR. OLLIVANDER (2010)
Set: 10217
See page 52

IGOR KARKAROFF (2005)
Set: 4768
See page 68

VIKTOR KRUM (2005)
Set: 4768
See page 69

VIKTOR KRUM (2005)
Set: 4762
See page 72

PEEVES (2001)
Sets: 4705 • 4709
See page 27

GRYFFINDOR KNIGHT (2001)
Set: 4709
See page 26

GRYFFINDOR KNIGHT (2010)
Set: 4842
See page 33

CHESS QUEEN (2001)
Set: 4704
See page 61

MARAUDER'S MAP STATUE (2004)
Set: 4751
See page 34

TROLL (2002)
Set: 4712
See page 56

MERPERSON (2005)
Set: 4762
See page 72

DOBBY (2002)
Set: 4731
See page 17

DOBBY (2010)
Set: 4736
See page 17

GRINGOTTS GOBLIN (2002)
Set: 4714
See page 54

GRIPHOOK (2002)
Set: 4714
See page 54

GRINGOTTS GOBLIN (2010)
Set: 10217
See page 55

GRINGOTTS GOBLIN (2010)
Set: 10217
See page 55

Like many LEGO minifigures since Professor Quirrell (2001), Fenrir has a double-sided head. He bares his teeth, as here, or frowns.

WHITE SKELETON (2003)
Sets: 4757 • 4766
See page 76

BLACK SKELETON (2005)
Set: 4766
See page 76

BLACK-AND-GREEN SKELETON (2005)
Set: 4766
See page 76

DEATH EATER (2005)
Set: 4766
See page 75

DEATH EATER (2007)
Set: 5378
See page 75

DEATH EATER (2011)
Set: 10217

BELLATRIX LESTRANGE (2010)
Set: 4840
See page 75

DEMENTOR (2004)
Sets: 4753 • 4757 • 4758 • 10132
See page 75

DEMENTOR (2010)
Set: 4842
See page 75

TOM RIDDLE (2002)
Set: 4730
See page 75

VOLDEMORT (2005)
Set: 4766
See page 74

VOLDEMORT (2010)
Set: 4842
See page 74

FENRIR GREYBACK (2010)
Set: 4840
See page 75

Index

Main entries are highlighted in bold.

DK

LONDON, NEW YORK, MUNICH,
MELBOURNE, AND DELHI

Senior Editor Elizabeth Dowsett
Editor Shari Last
Designer Owen Bennett
Managing Art Editor Ron Stobbart
Publishing Manager Catherine Saunders
Art Director Lisa Lanzarini
Associate Publisher Simon Beecroft
Category Publisher Alex Allan
Production Controller Man Fai Lau
Production Editor Clare McLean

Additional design for DK by Dan Bunyan

First published in the United States in 2011 by
DK Publishing
375 Hudson Street
New York, New York 10014

11 12 13 14 15 10 9 8 7 6 5 4 3 2 1
181145—04/11

Page design copyright © 2011 Dorling Kindersley Limited.

LEGO, the LEGO logo, the Brick and the Knob configurations, and the Minifigure
are trademarks of the LEGO Group. Copyright ©2011 The LEGO Group.
Produced by Dorling Kindersley Limited under license from the LEGO Group.

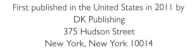
Discover more at
www.dk.com
www.LEGO.com
www.warnerbros.com

HARRY
POTTER

2001 uniform torso
with Gryffindor badge

Wheelbarrow
for Hogwarts
Quidditch equipment

Smirk

Remembrall

DRACO
MALFOY

FLYING LESSON (SET 4711)

Acknowledgments

Dorling Kindersley would like to thank Melanie
Swartz, Victoria Selover, Elaine Piechowski, and
Ashley Bol at Warner Bros., and also Stephanie
Lawrence, Randi Sørensen, and Anette Kaehne
Høgh at the LEGO Group, and J. K. Rowling.

The author would like to thank Henrik
Saaby Clausen, Chris Bonven Johansen,
Bjarke Lykke Madsen, Gitte Thorsen,
Luis F. E. Castaneda, Martin Fink,
Nicholas Groves, Sven Robin

Kahl, and Hans Henrik Sidenius at the LEGO
Group for their time and enthusiasm; and
Jonathan Smith and Loz Doyle at TT Games
Publishing for supplying information about the
computer game.

PICTURE CREDITS
All images supplied by the LEGO Group,
except for: Images on pages 82–85 originally
produced for the videogame LEGO® Harry
Potter™: Years 1–4, developed by Traveller's
Tales and produced by TT Games Publishing.

"PlayStation", "PS3", "PS2", "PSN", "PlayStation
Portable", "PlayStation 2", "PlayStation 3",
PlayStation 2 Logo, PSP Logo, PlayStation
Symbols Logo, PlayStation Network, PS3 Logo,
"DUALSHOCK", and "PS one" are trademarks
or registered trademarks of Sony Computer
Entertainment Inc. All rights reserved.
Microsoft, Xbox, Xbox LIVE, the Xbox logos,
and Xbox 360 are trademarks of the
Microsoft group of companies.